Betty Neels sadly passed away in 2001. As one of our best-loved authors, Betty will be greatly missed, both by her friends at Mills & Boon and by her legions of loyal readers around the world. Betty was a prolific writer and has left a lasting legacy through her heartwarming novels, and she will always be remembered as a truly delightful person who brought great happiness to many.

This special collection of Betty's best-loved books, are all available in Large Print, making them an easier read on your eyes, and ensuring you won't miss any of the romance in Betty's ever-popular novels.

The Betty Neels Large Print Collection

ENCHANTING SAMANTHA

BY

BETTY NEELS

MILLS & BOON®

First published in Great Britain 1973
Large Print Edition 2006
Harlequin Mills & Boon Limited,
Eton House, 18-24 Paradise Road,
Richmond, Surrey TW9 1SR

ISBN-13: 978 0 263 19323 7
ISBN-10:   0 263 19323 3

Set in Times Roman 16½ on 18 pt.
16-1106-50039

Printed and bound in Great Britain
by Antony Rowe Ltd, Chippenham, Wiltshire

CHAPTER ONE

IT WAS half past five on a cold February morning, and Clement's Hospital, behind its elaborate red brick Victorian façade, was already stirring, and this despite the edict from someone at the summit of the nursing profession that no patient should be aroused before six o'clock. An edict which the night nurses had, for a very long time, decided was a laughable impossibility, probably thought up, declared the younger and more frivolous of their number, by some dear old soul who still thought of nurses as ministering angels, gliding from bed to bed, turning pillows and smoothing brows while a vast number of underlings did the work, while in fact they were a band of understaffed, highly skilled young women who knew all about intensive care and cardiac arrest and electrolytes. True, the ward lights always went on at the precise hour allowed, shining out on to the grimy streets of one of the less

5

fashionable quarters of London, but long before that on this particular morning, stealthy
movement had been going on for an hour or
more in Women's Surgical, for it was operation day, which meant the preparation of those
ladies who were on Sir Joshua White's list, and
as most of them had wakened early despite
their sleeping pills the night before, the very
early morning cup of tea they were allowed
was immediately offered before the business of
cleansing the patients, clothing them in theatre
gowns and long woollen stockings, and in the
case of the first patient due in theatre at half
past eight sharp, removing anything from her
person to which the anaesthetist might take exception.

And now the last of them had been attended
to and those who were able were left to sit in
a cosy circle, enjoying a bloodcurdling and
quite inaccurate chat about their various in-
sides. They spoke in whispers, of course, because most of the other patients were still
asleep, but Staff Nurse Samantha Fielding,
carefully plaiting her patient's pepper-and-salt
hair behind the nearest cubicle curtains, caught

a word here and there, just as her ear, tuned in to the various noises, however slight, which she might expect to hear on the ward, caught the stealthy tread of her junior nurse, Dora Brown, who was creeping from locker to locker, laying down washing bowls with the stealth of hard-earned experience, putting soap and flannel and towel within reach of the sleeping patients. Samantha glanced at the clock at the far end of the ward. There was still twenty minutes to go before the lights could go on. She would have time to write the report for Sister before that lady came to do her final round, as well as start the wash-out on the second theatre case. The medicine round could be quickly done, and that only left the Kardex to be written up and then the hundred and one jobs listed in her head.

She smiled down at the elderly face on the pillow—a wrinkled face, still grey from shock, almost ugly. Indeed it seemed unlikely that the patient had ever been pretty, but it was a good face all the same and Staff Nurse Fielding liked it. The poor woman had been admitted just before midnight with badly burned hands, and although she had been sedated she had had a bad night despite all that could be done for her. But now she had been gently bathed and tidied up and her hands in their sterile plastic envelopes disposed side by side on the bed-cover. Second degree burns, the Registrar had said, which they had cleaned up in theatre before starting the Bunyan-Stannard treatment. Samantha had been irrigating them at intervals during the night; she did it once more now, deploring the fact that the patient could neither speak nor understand English. She had been brought to Clement's for the simple reason that when she had been found, lying before the exploded gas oven, all she had been able to say was the name of the hospital, and the police and ambulance men, struggling to make themselves understood, had brought her in, hopeful that there would be someone at Clement's who knew her. But no one did, nor had anyone succeeded in understanding the few muttered words the old lady uttered from time to time.

She had been alone in the house when the accident happened; the police had been called by the housemaid next door, who, curious to know who had come to live in a house which had stood empty for some time, had been standing on the area steps and had heard the bang.

Samantha smiled once again and nodded encouragingly as she popped a thermometer under her patient's tongue and took her pulse, both up, she noted; probably the poor old thing was wondering what would happen to her. She patted an arm and sped down the ward to the kitchen, fetched a feeder of tea and gave it to her with the gentle expertise of long practice.

She had finished the report with seconds to spare before Night Sister made her brief appearance on the ward and was taking down a drip when Brown appeared at her elbow to whisper: 'There's a man outside, Staff.'

'Good luck to him,' said Samantha absently, taking out the cannula with careful fingers and covering the tiny puncture with a strip of plaster.

Brown giggled. 'He wants to see the old lady—the one with the burns.'

Samantha laid the drip paraphernalia on the trolley and prepared to wheel it away. 'Tell him to wait, will you? He can't come in until you've finished the BP round and I simply must repack Mrs Wheeler's dressing.' Her eye fell on the clock. 'Oh, lord—just as we were getting on so nicely...'

She was packing Mrs Wheeler's leaking dressing when Brown appeared again. 'He says he'll be glad if you could be as quick as possible,' she added. 'He's ever so romantic-looking, Staff.'

Samantha muttered rudely under her breath and picked up her dressing tray. 'No one,' she stated repressively, 'is romantic-looking at this hour of the morning. He'll have to wait while I wash my hands. Have you finished the round?'

Brown nodded.

'Then pull any curtains that are necessary, will you?' she sighed. 'I suppose he'll have to come in, but it couldn't be a more awkward time.'

She disposed of the tray, washed her hands and marched briskly down the ward, a small, pleasantly plump figure, her cap perched very precisely on the top of her neatly piled brown hair, a frown marring a face, which, while by no means pretty, was pleasant enough, with hazel eyes fringed with short thick lashes, a nose turned up at its end and a mouth which though a little too large, could smile delightfully.

There was no sign of a smile now, though, as she charged silently through the swing doors and came to an abrupt halt by the man sitting on the radiator under the landing window—a large man, she saw, as he rose to his feet, towering over her. He was wearing a bulky car coat and she could see leather gloves stuffed anyhow into its pockets, she could also see that he was dark-haired, craggy-faced and handsome with it, and had grey eyes of a peculiar intensity. All these things she saw within a few seconds, having been trained to observe quickly, accurately and without comment. Before he could speak Samantha said: 'Good morning—I'm glad you've come; you know the patient, I take it? We don't know anything about her and we haven't been able to talk to her at all—she must feel terrible about it, poor soul. You've come at a very awkward time, but at least you're here now. If you would come into the office now and let me have her particulars, you could go and see her for a few minutes afterwards—the ward's closed, but just for once... Are you her son?'

His straight black brows rose an inch. 'My dear good girl, how you do chat—were you learning all that off by heart while I waited?' He had followed her to the office door and held it open for her to go inside. 'No, I'm not her son, just a very old friend.' His voice was deep and faintly amused and Samantha, still smarting from his first remark, sat down at the desk and waved him to a chair, explained with commendable brevity the nature of the pa-tient's injuries and asked:

'Could you tell me if she lives at the address where she was found? 26, Minterne Square, SW8.'

The chair, not built for comfortable sitting in by heavy-weights, creaked alarmingly as he crossed his very long legs. 'Yes, temporarily.'

Samantha wrote. 'Has she an occupation?'

'Er—housekeeper.'

She eyed him without favour. 'Could you help a little more, do you think? I'm very busy. Her name and has she relations or any friends to whom we can apply? And does she live alone and how old is she?'

He smiled lazily. 'She is sixty-nine, I think. How old are you?'

'That's my business,' she snapped tartly, 'and will you please…'

'Ah, yes. Her name is Klara Boot,' he stopped to spell it. 'She is a Dutchwoman, here for a short period to act as housekeeper at the house where she was found. She arrived only yesterday evening, and through an unfortunate chance I was delayed from meeting her. She speaks no English.'

Samantha looked up from her form, pen poised. 'Oh, I see, she lets rooms or something of that sort?'

He smiled faintly. 'Something of that sort,' he agreed. 'She has no relations to the best of my knowledge, so if there is anything needed for her, perhaps I could be told.' He stood up. 'And now if I might see her for a few minutes.'

Samantha felt inclined to take umbrage at his tone, but perhaps he had been up all night like she had and wasn't feeling very amiable. She got up and led the way to the ward, saying at the door: 'You'll come again? Day Sister will want to see you—have you a telephone number?'

He grinned. 'Now we are making strides— we might even arrange a date.'

She lost her breath and caught it again with an angry snort. 'Well, really—' she began, and then, at a loss for words, walked ahead of him down the ward, past the highly interested patients, to where the old lady lay. As she pulled the cubicle curtains back he put two hands on her waist, lifted her effortlessly on one side and strode past her to bend over the bed and greet the patient in the gentlest of voices in some language she couldn't make head or tail of. Samantha watched the elderly face light up, break into a smile and then dissolve into tears, but when she stepped forward, the man stopped her by saying:

'Thank you, dear girl, don't let me stop you from finishing your work.'

She contented herself with a cold: 'Ten minutes, if you please, and not a minute more,' before she stalked away. A rude and arrogant man, she fumed, even though his voice had held unmistakable authority. Too late she remembered that she had no idea who he was. He had mentioned being an old friend—possibly a lodger of some years' standing with the old lady. Perhaps she had moved house and he with her—in that case surely there would have been other lodgers? She started on the medicine round, still cross because he had called her 'dear girl' with an off-hand patronage which she found quite insulting. On an impulse she went to the desk and telephoned the Surgical Night Sister; let him try and patronize that formidable lady if he could—it was unfortunate that she wasn't to be found, and as it turned out it would have been pointless, for when Samantha, after exactly ten minutes, went to remind the visitor that he should go, he was nowhere to be found; he must have gone, very silently indeed, while her back was turned.

She explained it all to Sister Grieves when that lady came on duty at eight o'clock, and then sped away to the dining room for her breakfast, a meal which didn't take very long to eat, for it was the end of the month and she hadn't much money left. Tea and toast and butter—but as her companions at table were eating the same rather dull fare it didn't seem so bad. Besides, she lived out, in a flat shared with three other nurses, all at the moment on day duty, and they had become astonishingly clever at stretching the housekeeping money; there would be a nourishing stew that evening when Samantha got up, and before she went to bed she would make coffee, and there were plenty of biscuits. She thought longingly of her nights off, still three days away, when she could, since it was pay day, go home to her grandparents and eat all she wanted.

'You're quiet, Sam,' observed Pat Donovan from Men's Medical. 'Did you have a grotty night?'

Samantha spread the last slice of toast. 'Not too bad...' Before she could enlarge on this statement Dorothy Sellars from the Accident

Room chipped in: 'Did you find out anything about that dear old duck we sent up with the burned hands?'

Samantha nodded and said with a mouth full of toast: 'She had a visitor at six o'clock—a man. She's Dutch, some sort of housekeeper—comes from one of those uppercrust squares in Knightsbridge.'

'Was the man upper-crust too?' asked Pat flippantly.

Samantha considered. 'Yes, he was rude too. He said he was an old friend—I daresay he lodges with her or something of the sort, he was a bit vague.' She pushed back her chair. 'I'm off, see you all tonight.'

The flat she shared was a bare five minutes' walk from Clement's; the top floor of what must have been at one time a large family house, complete with subterranean kitchens and several roomy attics. It was let out in furnished flats now, and besides Samantha and her friends, who lived under the roof, there were seven other occupants, not counting old Mr Cockburn who owned the place and lived in the transformed basement kitchens, with their windows giving a sideways view of everyone who went in or came out. He was a nice old man, born and bred in the district and with a soft spot for the four young nurses living in his attics, a soft spot partly engendered by his theory that if he treated them right, if and when he needed to go to hospital—which the Lord forbid—they would treat him right too. A form of insurance, as it were.

Samantha waved to him as she climbed the steps. She was tired and it was a cold, grey morning. She had no fancy for a brisk walk, nor for the lengthy bus ride which would take her from this plebeian area of the city to its more fashionable shopping streets. She yawned widely as she toiled up the last of the stairs and unlocked their flat door.

It was unexpectedly pleasant inside—small and shabbily furnished, it was true, but they had three bedrooms between them as well as a sitting room, a minute kitchen and a bathroom with what Mr Cockburn optimistically and erroneously called 'constant 'ot'.

She went along to the small room she had to herself because she was on night duty and flung off her coat and gloves. The other three were on duty until five o'clock that afternoon, which meant she would be able to sleep undisturbed all day if she wished. She donned the communal apron hanging behind the kitchen door, switched on the radio and began to tidy the flat, whistling cheerfully in time with the music while she got out the carpet sweeper and found a duster. They were fair about sharing the chores of their little home; whoever was on night duty tidied up in the morning, washed the breakfast things and laid the table for supper, and whoever was off duty during the day prepared the evening meal and did the ironing. The shopping they shared.

Today the other three could share the chores between them. Samantha, having done her quota, undressed and wandered along to the bathroom, where she found, most satisfyingly, enough hot water to fill the bath almost full. She lay in it, almost asleep, wondering about the stranger who had visited the old lady that morning. A sudden memory of his large, firm hands on her waist as he had shifted her out of his path disturbed her so much that she got out of the bath long before the water had cooled and set about getting to bed in the shortest space of time. She was really very tired, she told herself, refusing to admit that she found her thoughts of the man disquieting. 'Probably because I dislike him so much,' she mumbled as she pulled the blankets over her head and allowed sleep to take over.

She was awakened by Sue Blane bearing a mug of tea and the news that supper would be ready in half an hour, and although her first involuntary thought was of the man who had come to the ward that morning, she swept it aside impatiently, gulped down her tea, dressed, pinned up her hair, added a modicum of make-up because it was a waste on night duty, anyway, and joined her fellow tenants round the supper table. Sue worked on Women's Medical, the other two, Joan and Pam, slaved away their lives, as they informed everyone, in the Children's Unit under a martinet of a Sister who had the manner and visage of an updated Miss Betsy Trotwood, only instead of disliking donkeys, she disliked young nurses. Samantha ate her stew and laughed at her friends' latest backslidings, and forgot all about her early morning visitor.

And there was no time to think of anything else but work when she reached the ward—there were the operation cases to settle after she had taken the report from Sister, they needed comforting and reassurance and lifting gently into the right position in which to sleep, and calm brief explanations—already given several times during the day—as to why they weren't quite themselves. It was amazing, Samantha thought, as she explained a drip to a peevish elderly lady who had taken exception to it, how dreamlike life appeared to the various ladies who had visited the operating theatre that day; a merciful state of affairs which she took care to prolong with the almost unnoticed jab in each patient's arm as they were settled for the night, so that they relaxed and slept.

Juffrouw Klara Boot needed a good deal of attention too, although her hands were doing as well as could be expected. Samantha irrigated them, made her as comfortable as possible and while Brown gave the old lady a drink, went away to prepare an injection for her too, for her kind eyes had noticed the drawn look on her patient's face, although it had lighted up with a cheerful smile when Samantha expressed admiration for the flowers on the bedtable and the pretty shawl round Juffrouw Boot's shoulders.

It was a pity that neither could understand what the other was saying, a fact which didn't stop Samantha chatting away as she worked, for surely the dear soul would feel less lonely if someone talked to her, even in a foreign tongue. She popped in her needle and shot the contents of the syringe expertly into Juffrouw Boot's arm, patted her shoulder in a motherly fashion, and slid away to help Brown with old Mrs Stone, who was deaf, ninety and not surprisingly, crotchety to boot, and all the while she was helping her companion to settle Mrs Stone, she was remembering the way Sister Grieves had bridled with pleasure as she recounted how Juffrouw Boot's visitor had been to see her—that he hadn't been rude to her was very apparent from her smiles—on the contrary, if Sister's expression was to be believed.

Samantha, who had almost burst with curiosity, had managed not to ask any questions about him, and Sister, while full of his charm, told her nothing which she didn't already know—and that was very little.

She had been to her own midnight meal and Brown had only been gone to hers for ten minutes or so when she sat down at Sister's desk and pulled the Drugs Book towards her and began to make her neat entries, her ordinary little face absorbed. She was disturbed almost immediately, however, by the opening of the ward door to admit Sir Joshua White, accompanied by her early morning visitor of the day before. Both gentlemen were in the full glory of white tie and tails and Samantha, getting to her feet, eyed them uncertainly. They had been to some function or other, she had no doubt, but what wind of fortune had brought them to the ward at this time of night? and why was this man with the senior consultant surgeon of Clement's? There was nothing amiss with Juffrouw Boot—the obvious common denominator with both men—for Jack Mitchell, the Registrar, had told her so when he had done his late evening round. And this wretched man was staring at her now with a look of amusement on his face which annoyed her out of all proportion to the circumstances.

Sir Joshua had reached her by now, nodded a cheerful greeting and said, his usually booming voice suitable muffled out of deference to the snores around them: 'Juffrouw Boot—is she asleep, Staff Nurse?'

'I hope so, sir.' Samantha's voice was polite, but her look dared him to wake the poor old thing.

He ignored the look. 'We'll be very quiet,' he promised her, and when she looked enquiringly at his companion: 'Ah, yes—this is Doctor ter Ossel. Our patient is his housekeeper.'

So that solved that little mystery. She gave the Dutch doctor a cold glance, said 'How do you do?' just as though they hadn't already met, and led the way up the ward to the patient's bed. Its occupant was asleep. At a sign from Sir Joshua, Samantha shone her torch on the envelopes enshrouding the burnt hands and the two men bent to examine them, and because she hadn't got the torch's beam exactly where he wanted it, Doctor ter Ossel put out a large hand to correct it. There was really no need for him to keep his firm grip over her own hand and it disturbed her very much that she should find such pleasure at his touch.

Presently they all went back down the ward once more, to Sister's desk, where Sir Joshua silently put out a hand for Juffrouw Boot's chart. Samantha waited patiently while the two men muttered and murmured together, until at last the older man wrote his fresh instructions and handed them back to her. They didn't stay after that; Sir Joshua wished her a civil good night and Doctor ter Ossel offered her a mocking one. She watched their disappearing backs—the Dutchman's so very broad—as they crossed the landing to the stairs, and decided that she disliked him very much.

The night was busy; Samantha escaped to breakfast thankfully, gobbled it in company with such of her friends as shared her table and set off for the flat. One more night's duty and she would be free for four days, the delightful thought quickened her steps and made her ha-

zel eyes shine—even a note left by her flat-
mates asking her to do the shopping before she
went to bed couldn't sour her pleasure.

She skipped round the flat, tidying up before
rather perfunctorily doing something to her
washed-out face. It was raining, a faint drizzle—she could wear her raincoat with its hood
up and not bother with her hair. She brushed
it out rather carelessly, tied it back and bundled
it away anyhow, then caught up the shopping
basket, raided the housekeeping kitty on the
mantelpiece, snatched up the shopping list
thoughtfully made out for her and dashed
down the three flights of stairs and through the
house door, waving automatically to Mr
Cockburn, whose face she could see, peering
sideways through his window.

There wasn't much shopping to do, as a
matter of fact; bread, a cauliflower to make a
cauliflower cheese for their suppers, four tubs
of yoghourt to follow it, some tea and butter
and more biscuits because they were quite
cheap and filled one up, and a tin of milk in
case an unexpected visitor should call for coffee. Having purchased these mundane articles

she paused for a long moment outside a flower shop and looked longingly at the daffodils and tulips in its window; several bunches would make the flat look quite beautiful. She opened her purse and counted the money inside and then closed it quickly, but she still went on looking. She was standing there when Doctor ter Ossel spoke.

'Good morning, Miss Fielding, do you intend to buy some flowers?'

She had whizzed round with the speed of a top. 'No,' she told him breathlessly, 'no. They—they die so quickly, it wouldn't be worth it.'

'Worth what?' he asked in such a gentle voice that she forgot for the moment that she didn't like him and was intent only on hiding from him the fact that she couldn't afford them.

'I like to see them growing,' she said after a pause.

'Let me take your basket.' And he had it before she could think of a good reason why he shouldn't. Too late she said, 'Oh, no—it doesn't matter—I mean, I'm only going back to the flat, it's no distance...'

'In that case, I'll give you a lift,' he told her.

She looked round her. There were several cars pulled into the curb of the slightly shabby little shopping centre. Samantha looked at them each in turn and then at him. 'It's very kind of you, but I'd rather walk.'

She was sorry she had said that, for he said instantly: 'Ah, the brush-off,' and his voice wasn't gentle any more and he was smiling with faint mockery. 'Just the same, I should like a few minutes with you—about Klara.'

The mockery wasn't faint now, it was very real; she went red under the gleam in his grey eyes and said stiffly: 'Very well,' and found herself walking beside him. When he stopped by a dark blue Rolls-Royce Merlin she did her best not to look surprised, but her ingenuous face wore such an eloquent look of enquiry that her companion said carelessly: 'I travel a good deal,' and as though he considered that sufficient, opened the door and bade her get in and make herself comfortable.

Samantha allowed her tired young bones to relax against the soft leather of the seat. How could one help but be comfortable? If it had been anyone else beside her but Doctor ter Ossel, she would have said so; as it was she gave him directions in a polite and wooden voice, and as he pulled away from the curb asked: 'What was it you want to know about Juffrouw Boot?'

She saw the thick eyebrows lift. 'My dear young woman, am I to be expected to tell you at this very moment? I think that I should be allowed a few minutes' quiet in which to do that, don't you? Your flat, perhaps?'

She cast him a suspicious glance. 'How did you know that I live out?'

He looked vague. 'Ah—do you know, I really cannot remember. Is this the street?'

'Yes.' There was no point in saying more; Morecombe Street was such that the less said about it the better; it was respectable, but it had seen more prosperous days. The doctor drew up outside the house and got out without haste and opened Samantha's door, collected her basket and then trod, without being asked, up the steps to the shabby front door. He even had the temerity to lift a hand in greeting to old Mr Cockburn, watching them with great interest from his window.

With key poised at her own front door, Samantha hesitated. 'Oh, yes,' he told her blandly before she could frame the polite request that he should say what he wanted to and be gone, 'I'll come in now I'm here.'

She led the way through the minute hall and into the sitting room, where he put the basket down and looked around him with leisurely interest.

'We like living out of the hospital,' she stated defensively, just as though he had made some derogatory remark about his surroundings. And instantly wished she hadn't spoken, because the eyebrows flew up once more although he said nothing, just stood there, dwarfing his surroundings and looking at her.

The rules of hospitality were too strong for her. 'Would you like a cup of coffee?' she asked him, and added dampeningly: 'It's Nescafé.'

He smiled at her and her heart flipped against her ribs because it was the smile he had given the old lady when he had visited her; kind and reassuring. 'That will be nice, but don't you go to bed?'

'Yes, but I always have coffee first.' She waved a small, sensible hand at the only real armchair the room contained. 'Do sit down.'

They were half way through their coffee when he said abruptly: 'I have to return to Holland for a day or so very shortly. I should be grateful if you would buy fruit and so on for Klara—and anything else she might fancy. I'll see that she has a list of likely things on her locker with appropriate translations; she can point out what she wants.'

He smiled again with a charm which caused her to smile back at him.

'She likes you, you know, she says you have a beautiful face.'

Her smile faded although she didn't look away from him. 'That's not true,' she told him, and was deeply mortified when he agreed: 'No, I know it's not, but I know exactly what Klara means.' He got up. 'I'll not keep you out of

your bed any longer, and thanks for the coffee.' He stuffed a hand into his pocket and
drew out some notes and put them on the table.
'I hope this will be enough.'

Samantha eyed the money. 'It's far too
much,' she told him roundly. 'Half of that...'

He smiled. 'Spend what you need,' was all
he said. 'I'll see myself out. Sleep well.'

For a large man he moved with a good deal
of speed. She heard the front door close while
she was still framing a suitable goodbye sentence.

Although she was so tired, she didn't sleep
very well, being disturbed by dreams which
she dismissed as absurd. It was, she told herself as she rose long before her usual time to
make herself a cup of tea, because Doctor ter
Ossel had been the last person she had seen
before she went to bed that she had dreamed
so persistently of him. She wandered into the
sitting room, trying to shake the memory of
him out of her still sleepy head, and found a
bowl crowded with daffodils and tulips on the

table and a note from Sue, who had been off duty during the afternoon.

It read simply. 'These came for you. Who's the boyfriend?'

CHAPTER TWO

THE NINE-THIRTY TRAIN from Waterloo to Weymouth was half empty. Samantha found a carriage in the front of the train and sank into a corner seat with a sigh of relief. It had been a rush to get to the station, but it was well worth it, she told herself. There were four days ahead of her and she intended to enjoy every minute of them. The last night of her duty had been busy and she had spent some of her precious free time shopping for Juffrouw Boot, who, just as the doctor had promised, had a list on her locker. It had been merely a question of pointing to which items she wanted in her own incomprehensible language while Samantha read them in the English written neatly beside them. She had taken upon herself to buy a few extra things too—more flowers, sweets, a bottle of perfumed eau-de-cologne, even a Dutch newspaper which she had discovered one morning and taken on duty that

34

night. She and Brown had rigged up the table so that Juffrouw Boot could see to read it; it meant taking her glasses on and off, of course, and turning the pages for her, but it had been well worth the trouble to see the pleasure on her face.

Samantha leaned her head back and closed her eyes. She had been paid; that meant that she had some money to give her grandmother, an undertaking of some delicacy because that lady had a good deal of old-fashioned pride, but once that was done, she might even, once she had paid her share of the flat's rent and the housekeeping and put some money aside to pay for her meals in the hospital, have sufficient over to buy one of those short jackets from Fenwick's—a brown one, she mused sleepily. She could wear it with her brown slacks and the tweed skirt she was so heartily sick of. She was trying to work out if there would be enough over to buy a thin sweater when she fell asleep. She slept until the train stopped at Southampton and woke to the suspicious stare of the woman seated opposite her; the woman didn't approve of her, that was evident; perhaps she felt that a girl should be wide awake at that hour of the morning after a sound night's rest. Samantha closed her eyes again, but this time she didn't sleep; Doctor ter Ossel's arrogant features superimposed themselves upon her eyelids and refused to go away. A bad-tempered man, she had no doubt, and far too outspoken; she was thankful that she had kept meticulous account of the money she had spent on his behalf, and left the change, together with a stiff little note, in Juffrouw Boot's locker. He hadn't said how long he was going to be away; almost certainly he would be gone again by the time she returned to duty. She felt a vague, unreasonable regret about this as she drifted off to sleep again.

The train filled itself at Bournemouth; she forced herself to wake up and look out of the window at the familiar scenery, so that she was quite alert by the time the train stopped, finally, at Weymouth.

Her grandfather was waiting for her, sitting in the driver's seat of the elderly Morris. He was an old man now and driving, because of his arthritis, was becoming increasingly difficult, but he always insisted on meeting her when she went home. She swung into the seat beside him, cast her case on to the back seat and embraced him with affection. He and her grandmother had looked after her since she had lost her parents at the age of twelve. They had given her a loving home, educated her well, although it had meant digging deep into their capital, and never grudged her a thing. Not that Samantha had ever asked for much; she had realized soon enough that there wasn't much money and what there was was being spent on her. That was why, now that she was earning her own living, she insisted on helping them each month; they didn't like it, but she suspected that they had very little besides their pension, although they were far too proud to tell her that.

'Lovely to see you, Grandpa,' she told the spare old gentleman as he drove through the town and out on to the Portisham road, and she went on to entertain him with some of the lighter aspects of hospital life until they reached the turning to Langton Herring, a narrow lane which meandered through fields and pleasant little copses before it arrived at the village; a mere cluster of houses about the church and almost at the end of the lane which wandered, its surface getting rougher at every yard, uphill and then down again until it ended at Chesil Beach and the coastguards' cottages.

Mr Fielding drove round the church, past the big open gate leading to the Manor, and stopped neatly before a small grey stone house with a very small garden before it. Its door stood open. Samantha flung out of the car and ran into its narrow passage, straight into the arms of her grandmother. Mrs Fielding was a little shorter than her granddaughter and a good deal plumper; they shared the same ordinary face and the same pretty twinkling eyes, but whereas her grandmother's hair was short and white and curly, Samantha's long brown hair was skewered rather severely above her slender neck.

They hugged each other, both talking at once, until Mr Fielding came in with her case and they all moved into the sitting room, where Samantha was regaled with several cups of strong tea and the cream of the local gossip was skimmed off until her grandmother looked at the clock and declared that it was high time that they had their dinner, and went off to the kitchen to dish up.

They all helped with the washing up in the small, pleasant kitchen and then, with her grandparents ensconced by the sitting room fire for their afternoon nap, Samantha went upstairs to her room. It was a small apartment, its window built out over the porch so that if she had a mind to, she could see anyone coming up the lane. But she didn't look out now. She unpacked the few things she had brought with her and put them tidily away and did her hair again, this time in a ponytail, and sat on the narrow bed, looking around her at the rather elderly furniture, the rosebud wallpaper and the little shelf of her favourite books by the bed. It was nice to be home again. She heaved a sigh of content and went quietly downstairs, laid her gifts of tobacco and chocolates on the kitchen table, took down an old tweed coat hanging behind the door, and went out. She walked past the church, stopped to say a word or two to the vicar when she met him, and then went briskly down the lane towards the sea, meeting no one else on the way. It was a dull afternoon and the water, when she reached it, looked dark and cold and the mean little wind blowing in over Chesil Beach made everything look very uninviting. Samantha turned and walked back, her hands in the pockets of her deplorable coat, frowning to herself, because for no reason at all, she was thinking about Doctor ter Ossel again.

It was the next morning, over breakfast, that Mrs Fielding mentioned casually that they had all been bidden to dinner that evening at the Manor.

'But, Granny,' said Samantha, astonished, 'we only go at Christmas and New Year and once or twice in the summer.'

Her grandmother looked vaguely puzzled. 'Yes, dear, I know, but I met Mrs Humphries-Potter a few days ago and she told me that she was on the way to visit us in order to invite us all for tonight. She was most particular about it—I can't imagine why, excepting she said that she hadn't seen you for a long time.'

'Christmas! I've nothing to wear!'

'Oh, I'm sure you have, darling—it's not a party, just us, I believe. That was a pretty dress you had on yesterday.'

Samantha eyed her grandmother with tolerant affection. A Marks & Spencer jersey dress, and she had had it for more than a year. But she could dress it up a bit, she supposed, there was that lovely belt someone had given her for Christmas and she had a decent pair of shoes somewhere. 'OK,' she agreed cheerfully, 'I'll wear that.'

They got out the car to go to the Manor, for although it was a very short drive, her grandfather wasn't much of a walker these days. This time Samantha drove, first packing the elderly pair into the back of the car and then, at her grandmother's agitated request, went back into the house to make sure that Stubbs, the cat, was safely indoors. They had had Stubbs for a long time now, he was part of the family, his every whim pandered to, and much thought given to his comfort. Samantha got into the driving seat at last, assured her companions that Stubbs was cosily asleep, and drove off up the lane, round the corner, through the open gate and up the winding drive, to park the car on one side of the sweep before the house.

The Squire, an elderly man, become rather stout with advancing years, came to meet them as Mrs Mabb, who did for the Humphries-Potters, opened the door. He was followed by his wife, a commanding lady of majestic aspect and possessing one of the kindest hearts in the district. She pecked Mrs Fielding's cheek in greeting and then did the same for Samantha, commenting as she did so that the dear child looked far too pale. The Squire kissed her too, rather more robustly, and slapped her in avuncular fashion as well, for they had known her since she was a small girl. Carried along on a burst of cheerful conversation, they crossed the hall and arranged themselves in a circle round the fire to drink their sherries and gin and tonics. Samantha was listening to Mrs Humphries-Potter's plans for the church bazaar, when that lady's rigidly coiffed head bent to a listening angle. 'There is the car,' she pronounced, and even as

Samantha framed the question: 'Whose car?' Mrs Mabb threw open the door with something of a flourish and Doctor ter Ossel walked in.

Under Samantha's startled gaze he greeted his host and hostess, was introduced to Mr and Mrs Fielding, and finally, to herself. The look he gave her was bland as they shook hands, faintly amused and tinged with an innocent surprise which she suspected wasn't innocent at all.

'We have already met,' he informed Mrs Humphries-Potter suavely, 'at Clement's, you know.'

His hostess smiled graciously. 'Of course—dear Sir Joshua.' She tapped the doctor playfully on his well tailored sleeve. 'If it hadn't been for him we should never have made your acquaintance or had the pleasure of your company here.'

'A mutual pleasure, Mrs Humphries-Potter.' His eyes rested briefly on Samantha, standing between them and wishing she wasn't. 'And what a strange coincidence that—er—Samantha should be here too.'

Samantha felt Mrs Humphries-Potter's hand on her shoulder. 'The dear child,' she said with real affection. 'We have known her for a good many years, for the Fieldings are neighbours of ours...' She broke off as the Squire came over with a drink for the newcomer and Samantha, with a wordless murmur, slipped away to join her grandmother. Presently the three gentlemen struck up a conversation, and Samantha, sitting between the two older ladies, listening with half an ear to their gentle criticisms of the latest books, the newest fashions and the terrible price of everything, had ample opportunity of studying Doctor ter Ossel. Apart from the fact that she disliked him, he was rather nice; a handsome man, tall and commanding and very sure of himself, and, she decided in a rather muddled fashion, very likeable, if one happened to like him—which she didn't, she apostrophized herself sharply, and just as well as it turned out, for she was quite sure that he didn't like her all that much, either.

But as the evening wore on she was bound to admit that he was allowing none of his true feelings towards her to show; indeed he was friendly in a cool kind of way, although he made no effort to single her out. He spent a good deal of time talking to Mrs Fielding, whose cosy chuckles and tinkling laugh bore tribute to the pleasure she was having in his company. Her granddaughter, listening to the Squire boring on about winter grazing and the price of animal foodstuffs, wished, quite unfairly, that her grandmother wasn't enjoying herself quite so much; it was ridiculous of her, old enough to know better, to succumb to the man's charm so easily.

'You're frowning, Sam,' the Squire interrupted himself to say. 'Perhaps you don't agree with me about this question of silage.'

Samantha's wits were quick enough behind her placid face. 'The Common Market countries—' she began, apropos of nothing at all and hoping that it might mean something to her companion.

It did. 'Clever girl,' he praised her, 'you're thinking of the price of beef...' He launched himself happily into a further explanation which only necessitated her saying: 'You don't

say,' or 'Yes, I see,' or 'Well, I never,' at intervals. She had turned her shoulder to her
grandmother and the doctor, but she could still
hear her grandmother's delighted chuckles.

They left soon after ten o'clock, and
Samantha, who was driving again, was deeply
mortified when she clashed the gears and put
the Morris into reverse by mistake, in full view
of the Squire and the doctor, who had come
out to see them off. It was dark except for the
powerful lights from the house; she had no
doubt that if she could have seen Doctor ter
Ossel clearly he would have been both amused
and mocking.

That her grandparents had enjoyed themselves was evident from their conversation
during the short drive home, and over their
bedtime cocoa Mrs Fielding remarked: 'I liked
that Doctor what's-his-name—Giles. Such a
nice young man, don't you think, Sam?'

Samantha was filling hot water bottles at the
sink. 'I don't know, Granny,' her voice was
prim. 'I suppose he's all right.'

Her grandmother spooned the sugar from
the bottom of her cup and gave her a bright

glance which she then turned upon her husband, ending it with a wink. He lowered a wrinkled eyelid himself and rumbled obligingly:

'Yes, yes—a very good sort of chap, I thought. Humphries-Potter tells me that he's considered very promising as a physician, too—does quite a bit of consulting work, I gather, and comes over here from time to time. Quite young, too.'

A bait to which Samantha rose. 'How young?' she wanted to know.

'Thirty-five,' declared her grandfather in an offhand manner. 'He has a practice in Haarlem, I'm told. Got his M. D. Cantab. too, as well as a fistful of Dutch degrees. Clever fellow.'

Samantha, washing cups and saucers, was thinking up a few careless questions to follow this interesting information, but her grandfather was a little too quick for her. He stood up and walked to the door.

'Well, I shall turn in,' he observed, and after kissing her, stumped upstairs, leaving her with her curiosity sufficiently aroused to prevent her from falling asleep for quite a long time.

She was up early, all the same, taking up tea to the old people, attending to Stubbs' wants, pottering round the little house, tidying up and getting breakfast, so that it was after that meal was finished and the remainder of the chores done that she was up in her room again, doing something to her face. The beds were made, the coffee hot on the side of the stove; there was little left to do. Samantha sat before the old-fashioned dressing table, not seeing her own reflection but Doctor ter Ossel's strong features. She closed her eyes upon it, brushed her hair into a shining brown curtain and tied it back with a ribbon. She was pulling at its loops when there was a knock on the front door and she poked her head out of the window to see who it was before going downstairs.

There were two people; Mrs Humphries-Potter and Doctor ter Ossel, and as that lady was already looking up at the window Samantha had opened, it was impossible to withdraw her head and pretend she wasn't there.

She called down politely: 'Good morning, I'm just coming,' and heard her grandfather going to open the door as she spoke.

In the kitchen she added two more cups and saucers to the coffee tray and carried it in the sitting room, where Doctor ter Ossel politely took it from her while Mrs Humphries-Potter exclaimed: 'Giles is so anxious to see the Beach, and I'm such a bad walker, as you know, so I hit on this perfectly splendid idea of Samantha acting as guide in my place. She knows this district so well and can answer any questions Giles might ask.'

She turned her head, crowned with a mud-coloured Henry Heath hat, and smiled at Samantha, who didn't smile back. 'I've a great deal to do,' she started to say. 'There's lunch to get ready and I was going to make some cakes…'

Her grandmother wasn't on her side, though. 'Nonsense, Sam,' she said quickly, 'you've done everything, I saw you with my own eyes, and the cakes can be made after lunch. You run along and enjoy yourself, dear.'

'I could always go alone,' interposed the doctor in a voice which somehow conveyed bravely concealed resignation at the prospect. 'I daresay there are plenty of books I can read to discover what I should want to know.' He turned his eyes upon Samantha and they were dancing with mirth. 'I shouldn't like to impose...'

She all but ground her teeth at him. 'I'll go and put a coat on,' she told him ungraciously, and fled upstairs, to fling on the old tweed coat, bundle her hair under its hood, snatch up some woolly mitts, and run downstairs again, her face a little pink with temper and some other feeling she refused to acknowledge.

It wasn't much of a morning; they walked briskly down the lane which led seawards under a sky covered with high grey cloud, while a fitful wind blew in their faces. The doctor, hatless and wearing a Burberry which emphasized the width of his shoulders as well as being gloved expensively in pigskin, didn't appear to notice the weather, however. He carried on a cheerful conversation about nothing in particular, to which Samantha contributed but little, answering with a determined politeness and a faint coolness of manner, for she had no intention of succumbing to his charm. She had no doubt, she told herself crossly, that if there had been another girl boasting the good looks she didn't have, he wouldn't have come near her that morning.

They had walked right down to the coast-guards' houses facing Chesil Beach itself, and she began to explain with meticulous thoroughness, as though she were a guide making something clear to a foreigner, that the Beach was seventeen miles long, that the stones at one end were much larger than those at the other, that if he chose to search, he might find Wolf's rock from Cornwall, Devon granite, quartz rock and banded rhyolite, that if he were interested there was no reason why he should not take one of the larger pieces home with him—people used them for paperweights. 'The Beach changes from day to day,' she went on, a little prosily. 'The tides…'

'Why do you dislike me?' He cut her off in full spate and left her openmouthed. 'Or rather, why will you not let yourself like me?'

She remembered to close her mouth while she sought for words. 'I—' she began, and then burst out with: 'What difference could it possibly make?' Her hazel eyes were bright with sudden rage. 'I don't know anything about you; I shan't ever see you again…'

He smiled faintly. 'But you don't enjoy my company? Come, let us be honest.'

She said wildly: 'But I've not been in your company—I don't…'

'Know me? Don't repeat yourself, Samantha. Perhaps given the opportunity, you might get to know me better.' He sounded so very sure of himself that she said instantly, not meaning a word of it: 'I have no wish to know you better—no wish at all. We'd better go back or you'll be late for your lunch.'

He appeared not in the least put out by this display of rudeness; they climbed the rough road again and began the walk back to the village, the doctor whiling away their journey with a discourse on igneous rock, lapilli, tuff and schist, and as she had never heard of any of these, she was forced to remain silent. At her grandparents' gate they came to a halt and she said awkwardly: 'Well, goodbye, Doctor ter Ossel.'

His cheerful goodbye in reply was vexing in the extreme; still more vexing was his remark: 'I'm going back to London tomorrow morning—such a pity I am unable to give you a lift—you don't return for another day, do you, but in any case, there is no point in mentioning it, is there, for I am sure that you would not have come with me, would you?' He went on blandly: 'One should never waste one's leisure in the company of someone one doesn't like.'

He had gone, walking unhurriedly up the lane, leaving her a prey to a variety of feelings, all muddled and none of them nice.

She spent the rest of the day indoors with the excuse that her grandmother's cushion-covers in the sitting room needed to be washed and ironed and it was just the day in which to do them. Her grandparents forbore from pointing out that a light drizzle was now falling and enquired discreetly as to her walk with the doctor. Samantha replied calmly that it had been nice, cold on the beach, though, and that Doctor ter Ossel was interested in a variety of stones, and before either of her listeners could ask, volunteered the information that he was returning to London the following morning.

She was upstairs making the beds when he called the next morning; she had peered out to see who it was at the door and had almost fallen over in her haste to get her head back inside again in case he should look up. Which he didn't, Samantha stood behind the curtain to see. She took a long time over the beds, telling herself that she didn't want to see him again, and was inordinately peeved when he left without anyone so much as calling up the stairs to tell her he was there, and when she went down after a suitable interval, Mrs Fielding mentioned placidly that she hadn't bothered her because he had only come in for a moment to say goodbye and had told them that he had already bidden her farewell after their walk the day before. 'Just fancy,' breathed her grandmother to no one in partic-ular, 'he's going back to Holland tonight, although he's going to see his poor housekeeper in Clement's first.'

And that, said Samantha silently, is that, adding for good measure: and a good thing too. It was probably the relief of knowing that she wouldn't meet him again which gave her such a curious sensation of emptiness; rather as though she had lost something.

But she hadn't lost anything; when she got back on duty two nights later, he was there on the ward, chatting up Sister Grieves, so that lady, usually so severe, was all smiles and pinkened cheeks. Samantha gave him an austere good evening and waited neatly by the desk, very clean and starched in her uniform, not a brown hair out of place, her eyes on Sister's animated face. They flew to Doctor ter Ossel's handsome countenance, though, when he said: 'Well, Samantha, I hope you left your grandparents well?'

She bristled; calling her Samantha in front of Sister, indeed! 'Perfectly well, thank you,' she assured him indignantly, and he gave the smallest of smiles as he turned back to Sister Grieves.

'Well, I won't keep you from your work, Sister. Good night, and many thanks, you have been more than kind.' He smiled at her. He turned to Samantha then and allowed the smile to become mocking. 'And good night to you Staff Nurse.'

It was Sister Grieves who answered him as he went away. Samantha had no words to say at all.

'I had no idea that you were on friendly terms with Doctor ter Ossel,' Sister Grieves remarked almost accusingly. It was the sort of question it was hard to answer without being downright rude; Samantha murmured something about his visits to Juffrouw Boot and didn't explain about her grandparents at all, so that Sister Grieves positively sizzled with curiosity as she gave the report.

The ward was full; Samantha nipped round, greeting the patients she knew and getting to know the new inmates of beds which had stood so briefly empty. It had not, thank heaven, been operating day, and although there were several ill patients there was nothing really dire. Night Sister did her round and Samantha gave out pills, medicines and where necessary, injections. By eleven o'clock the ward was quiet, more or less. Brown went to the kitchen to make coffee and Samantha went noiselessly to the desk and sat down to con the Kardex once more; she was a good nurse and careful; besides, when Brown came back with their drinks they would go over it together once more, so that the junior nurse, who was expected to plunge straight into work when she came on duty, knew as much as possible about the patients.

She was half way through the Kardex, conning Juffrouw Boot's notes, and paused to think about that lady; a nice old thing, she decided—she had become quite fond of her— with a good deal of courage and very grateful for anything which was done for her. She had learned a few words of English too; she could say yes and no and pain and bedpan, and it was remarkable what interesting conversations the nurses had with her when there was the time. She had taught Samantha a few Dutch words too while her hands were being treated during the night and had chuckled at her efforts. Samantha was glad to know that her hands were healing nicely. She flipped over the card and heard the door behind her open.

'Thank heaven,' she whispered. 'I thought you were never coming.'

'Now that is quite the nicest thing you have said to me.' Doctor ter Ossel's whisper was in her ear; he had bent down over her chair and she turned sharply to find his grey eyes within an inch or so of her own. A little short of breath, she managed: 'Grandmother told me that you had gone to Holland.'

'Quite right. Now I'm back—to see some-one.'

Samantha got up with as much dignity as space permitted, for he hadn't moved an inch. 'If you've come to see Juffrouw Boot, it's rather late, she'll be asleep.'

'I saw Klara this evening.'

'Then who?'

'Ah—the someone. I've seen her. I popped in while passing merely.'

'Oh.' Considering how much she disliked him, the feelings engendered by this remark made no sense. Samantha stared up at him,

wishing she knew who the someone was—
there were pretty girls galore in the hospital,
and several young and attractive doctors besides. She was wondering how she could find
out when Brown came creeping in through the
door with two mugs of coffee. She stopped
when she saw the doctor, spilled some of the
coffee down her apron and whispered: 'Oh—
do you want some coffee too?'

He took the mugs from her and set them
down on the desk, his smile earning him an
answering one from her round young face.
'No, thanks, my dear, I'm just going. Keep an
eye on this staff nurse of yours, will you? I
don't believe she's ever heard that one about
all work and no play...' He nodded briskly to
the pair of them and slid his bulk soundlessly
through the door.

Brown let out a noisy breath. 'Well, whatever did he mean, Staff?'

'I haven't the faintest idea,' said Samantha
tartly.

'He's foreign, remember; I daresay he's got
his metaphors mixed.' She wasn't sure if that
was the right expression, she had a sneaking

doubt that it hadn't been a metaphor at all, but it sounded most convincing and Brown, who was a good girl but not very bright, didn't appear to question it. They drank their coffee and conned the report and in the welter of questions and answers, forgot all about their visitor—or almost. As they got to their feet to do a ward round, Brown whispered: 'He's nice, isn't he, Staff—so romantic—he turns me on.'

Samantha picked up her torch, suddenly and surprisingly aware that to speak truth, he turned her on too, although she had no intention of admitting it. 'He's quite nice,' she agreed quenchingly, and was conscious of her companion's pitying glance; probably the girl considered her an old maid at twenty-four; she was, in all fairness, right.

It was during the following week that the ancillary staff of the hospital decided to go on strike, not all of them willingly. But as Betsy, the elderly ward maid, pointed out to Samantha when she came on duty to find the supper dishes still unwashed: 'It's not that I likes the idea, Staff—it's the money, they says it ain't enough.' She jerked a grubby thumb over her shoulder. 'Them poor cows in the ward, I'ates ter leave them.'

Samantha knew what she meant, even though her description of the ladies lying in the ward beds was hardly one she would have used herself, but old Betsy's heart was in the right place even if her mode of speech was a thought rough; she had been told not to work, but that didn't prevent her from stating her opinion of the situation. 'I'm not supposed to be 'ere, neither,' she confided. 'I just popped up to see 'ow yer was managing.' She made for the door. 'Well, ta-ta, ducks, be seeing yer.'

It wasn't too bad for the first couple of days; the nursing staff shared the extra work; the day nurses staying on later and going on duty earlier and the night staff doing the same, apportioning the washing up, the sweeping and dusting between them. It was when Sir Joshua White, doing his round a little early on the third morning and finding Samantha in the kitchen long after she should have been off duty, washing the endless cups and saucers while Sister Grieves vacuumed the ward floor, spoke his mind.

'You are two hours late off duty,' he pointed out to Samantha, quite unnecessarily. 'It is impossible for you to carry out your nursing duties and be a maid of all work at the same time—the patients are liable to suffer.'

'No, they aren't,' said Samantha, careless of her manners because she was half asleep and wanted her breakfast.

He studied her tired face through his gold-rimmed spectacles. 'No—I shouldn't have said that, I apologize, but you're going to be worn out, young lady. I shall have to think of something.'

He stalked away and she could hear him in the ward, surrounded by scurrying nurses trying to get the ward straight, addressing Sister in outraged tones, raising his voice a little because she still had the Hoover on.

That evening, when Samantha went on early so as to give a hand with the supper dishes, she went straight to the kitchen as usual, for Sister Grieves would be writing the report, and although the ward wasn't taking any fresh cases because there was no linen for the theatre, there was more than enough to do. She flung open the door to find Doctor ter Ossel at the sink while Sir Joshua, wielding a tea towel with the same assurance as he did his scalpel, dried up. Both gentlemen were in their shirtsleeves and both were smoking their pipes, so that the atmosphere, already damp and redolent of burnt toast, baked beans and the peculiar odour of washing up done on the grand scale, was enriched by volumes of smoke from one of the more expensive tobaccos.

'I told you that I would think of something,' Sir Joshua greeted her. 'Did you get any breakfast?'

'Well—I have a meal when I get to the flat. I sleep out, sir.'

He eyed her narrowly, made a rumbling noise in his throat and applied himself to the spoons and forks. It was Doctor ter Ossel who put his pipe down on the shelf above the sink and turned to ask: 'What sort of meal?'

Samantha was stacking the trolley ready for the evening drinks. 'Oh, tea and toast and marmalade, of course.'

He picked up his pipe again. 'Not enough—you'll lose weight.' He grinned at her and she felt her cheeks go red; her slight plumpness was something she was sensitive about—perhaps he thought of her as fat.

'And what about our little Nurse Brown?' he wanted to know. 'Does she live out too?'

Samantha shook her head. 'She's only eighteen.' She sounded almost motherly. 'She lives quite close by, so she goes home for breakfast and supper.'

She went to the shelves and picked up the Ovaltine, the Bengers, the Nescafé and the Horlicks and arranged them in an orderly row on the trolley. 'Shall I take over now?' she asked.

'Certainly not,' said Sir Joshua. 'As a married man, I have acquired the knack of wiping dishes of an evening, and as for Giles here, being still a bachelor, it's a splendid opportunity for him to learn a few of the more practical arts of marriage.'

He flung his damp tea towel into a corner of the kitchen and took the clean one Samantha thoughtfully handed him. 'We shall be here in the morning, Staff. I've arranged everything with Sister Grieves.'

She murmured her appreciation and went into the ward to give the hard-pressed day staff a hand, and presently, when Brown arrived, joined Sister at the desk.

It should have been a fairly easy night; no operation cases and six empty beds, but there were the tea towels to wash out and boil and the kitchen to clean up, because the day staff would have more than enough to do in the morning. She hadn't quite believed Sir Joshua when he had said that they would be there in the morning, but when she went into the kitchen to help Brown with the early teas, the two men were already there; the trolleys were ready, the kettles boiling, the tea in the pot and Doctor ter Ossel buttering bread with a casual speed which earned Samantha's instant admiration. She and Brown were able to go back to the ward and make beds for the first time in several days; they were even ready to go off duty on time and what was more, had done a sizeable amount of work for the day nurses. Samantha sent Brown on ahead and stopped to poke her head round the kitchen door. The men had gone, the day staff were already stacking the breakfast things which Sir Joshua's registrar had promised to wash presently. She yawned and pattered downstairs to the cloakroom, found her coat, tied a scarf over her untidy head without bothering to look in a mirror and left the hospital. She was tired, and what was more, very hungry. She would buy some bacon on the way to the flat and have a really good meal before washing out her uniform dress and ironing one for that evening—there were aprons too. She yawned again and almost choked on it; Doctor ter Ossel was standing on the pavement waiting for her.

'Breakfast,' he said crisply, and popped her into the Rolls at the curb, got in beside her and was driving away before she had the breath to say: 'You're mad—I mean, I'm going back to the flat, but I must buy some bacon...'

'You're too tired to cook,' he observed, 'and I like my bacon just so. We'll have breakfast somewhere and then you can go home to bed.'

'I can't—go out, I mean. Look at me, I'm still in my uniform under this coat and I haven't done my face or my hair, and I've a pile of washing to do.'

'Breakfast first,' he reiterated in the reasonable voice of a grown-up making a point with a refractory child. 'We'll discuss the washing later.' He turned to look at her. 'You look all right to me.'

He had turned into Kingsway and presently Aldwych and stopped now outside the impressive front of the Waldorf. It took Samantha a few seconds to grasp the fact that this was actually where he intended they should eat their breakfast. 'I can't go in there,' she expostulated strongly. 'You must be quite mad!'

He shook his head. 'Hungry, and so, I imagine, are you. They know we're coming and of course you can go inside.' He smiled suddenly and very kindly. 'You may dislike me, Samantha, but even so you can trust me, I hope. I promise you you need not feel uncomfortable.'

He got out and walked round the car and opened the door for her, tucked a hand under her elbow and walked her into the hotel.

And he was quite right, she discovered. She was whisked away to the powder room where, with the help of the sympathetic attendant, she improved her appearance considerably and, heartened by the result, joined the doctor in the foyer. They breakfasted alone in a small coffee room, waited upon by a fatherly personage, who pressed a substantial meal upon them without appearing to do so, and contrary to her expectations, Samantha wasn't aware of her appearance at all. Indeed, Doctor ter Ossel somehow managed to convey the impression—without saying a word—that she looked rather nice. She ate her way happily through porridge, bacon and eggs and toast and marmalade, while the doctor, keeping pace with her, contrived to entertain her with small talk which required the minimum of answers.

They didn't hurry; she felt wide awake again, she assured him, but when they got into the car again, she fell asleep in the middle of thanking him.

He wakened her gently when they reached the flat and she said at once in a sleep-thickened voice: 'You don't mind if I don't ask you in for coffee?'

'Not in the least, but I'm coming in all the same.'

And because she was so very sleepy she hardly heard him, but walked docilely up the steps with him. Half way up the doctor caught sight of Mr Cockburn's face at his window and stopped, giving Samantha a gentle push. 'Go on up—I'll be with you in a second.'

She nodded and when she reached the stairs, sat down on the bottom step and went to sleep again.

The doctor leant his large frame over the railings and tapped at Mr Cockburn's window, to have it instantly flung open.

''Ow do, cock,' said the old gentleman.

The doctor acknowledged this greeting with a grin. 'I take it that you have no objection to my going up to Miss Fielding's flat? She's quite exhausted.'

'You a doctor? I thought yer was. Course I don't mind—poor young thing, wore out, I bet, with all that extra work. Yer can go on up and my blessing, doc.'

Samantha hardly roused as he scooped her off the stairs and carried her up to the attics, although once, when he paused to take a breather on the second landing, she managed to tell him that she was too heavy for him—a remark which brought forth a reassuring laugh from him so that she felt quite justified in closing her eyes again.

In the flat, however, he set her on her feet. 'Wake up, dear girl,' he begged her. 'Go and take a bath and get into bed, and look sharp about it.'

Samantha blinked at him. 'I can't—I simply must iron some uniform for tonight.' She walked past him into the kitchen and he put out a long arm and turned her gently round and walked her out again. 'Bath,' he told her, 'and bed, in that order. I'll see to the ironing.'

Even half asleep she found this funny enough to laugh over. 'Of course you can't— and there are lots of things I have to do…'

'Forget them. Go to bed, Samantha.' He pulled her close and kissed her swiftly on her cheek. 'Sleep well.'

She had had really no intention of doing as he asked, but somehow she found herself undressing, bathing and tumbling into bed. The last thing she was conscious of was the faint, fresh smell of newly ironed cotton. Presumably the doctor was trying his hand at the ironing. If she hadn't been so very sleepy she would have laughed again.

And when she got up, greatly refreshed, that evening, it was to find that he had done much more than the ironing. The room was tidied, the table had been laid for supper, the potatoes had been peeled and put in a saucepan on the stove and he had left the tea tray ready. The other three girls, struggling in late and worn out, could hardly believe their eyes, and when Samantha tried to explain, they could hardly believe their ears either. She should have felt flattered, she thought, at their interest and curiosity as they loaded her with messages of gratitude to pass on to him when she saw him again—an event, they were all three sure, which would be soon.

CHAPTER THREE

THERE WAS no sign of Doctor ter Ossel that evening when Samantha got on duty; Sir Joshua was in the kitchen, but he was partnered by Jack Mitchell, who was making such heavy weather of the washing up that she felt forced to offer her help.

'He hasn't got the knack,' Sir Joshua explained, 'and if he doesn't improve pretty smartish he'll make some poor girl a rotten husband. Now Giles—he's a handy man with the dish mop.' He picked up a fistful of forks and began to dry them. 'Did you have a good breakfast?' he asked Samantha.

'Yes, thank you, sir. Gorgeous. Though I was so sleepy I didn't appreciate it as I should have done. Doctor ter Ossel was very kind—I didn't have the chance to thank him properly...'

Sir Joshua rose nicely to the bait. 'He's in Birmingham or Manchester or some such place,' he said vaguely, 'at some meeting or other.'

He dropped the tea towel he had been using on to the floor, rather as though he were in theatre, tossing away swabs, and put out his hand for a fresh one. Samantha put it into his hand, finished her trolley and went to find someone to give her the report. Sister was off, so it would be Margaret, a friend of hers; a quiet girl whose ambition was to be a Ward Sister as quickly as possible. She had been staffing on Women's Surgical for six months now and in another two or three hoped to be offered Men's Surgical in the new wing. Samantha found her now, conscientiously filling in forms. She pulled up a chair and sat down on the other side of Sister's desk in the office and asked her friend:

'Margaret, don't you want to get married?'

Margaret lifted her head briefly. 'Me? Not particularly. Why, do you?'

'Well, it might be rather fun,' said Samantha slowly. How crazy could a girl get, just because she had breakfast with a good-looking man who could afford to eat at the Waldorf?

She didn't like him either. She bent her head and examined her hands without seeing them—or did she like him after all?

'Well, ducky,' commented Margaret, slamming the forms into a drawer, 'go on, make a play for him, whoever he is. You may not be a raving beauty, but there's nothing wrong with the rest of you.'

Samantha glanced up briefly and spoke with elaborate casualness. 'Oh, it's no one in particular—I just asked. I'm not fired with ambition like you, Margaret.'

Her friend gave her a considered glance. 'You're doing very nicely as you are.' She opened the Kardex. 'I'll stay on for a bit when we've gone through the report; they've sent up a whole pile of paper sheets and what have you—I'll get them out of the way for you. They—whoever they are—say that this strike will be over in a few days and thank God for that, I'm sick of washing and ironing my uniform and I haven't an apron left.' Her eyes lighted upon Samantha's pristine appearance. 'I must say you're pretty good at it, though. Quite professional.'

Samantha glanced down at her person, a little pink. The doctor had done his ironing well, he must have worked very hard.

'Hey,' said Margaret, 'come out of your trance, Sam, and let's get this report rattled off. There's one in—stabbing—an emergency. We've had a policewoman here all day with pencil poised ready to take a statement. She went about an hour ago and the girl'll do— she's written up for Pethidine, for she's a bit of a handful... Now, bed one, Mrs Jeffs...'

They became immersed in the report.

It wasn't a quiet night at all; the patients didn't settle well and Nurse Brown upset a tin of Horlicks all over the kitchen floor and followed this regrettable action by falling downstairs with the bucket of refuse she was on her way to empty. The whole wing of the hospital re-echoed to the din, and while she, most fortunately, got off with a bruise or so, the refuse had flown in all directions. Volunteers amongst her friends on neighbouring wards, in rubber gloves and with their aprons pinned back, made short work of cleaning up the mess, but quiet though they were, it was enough to disturb some of the patients, who first wanted to know what the noise was, and having been told and urged to go to sleep again, declared that they could not, which meant creeping up and down the ward with cups of tea and hot milk and a great shaking up of pillows. And just as everyone had dropped off once more the girl with the stab wounds wakened, demanding to know in a loud voice where she was and why, and on being told, declared her intention of going home that very minute. Samantha, who had anticipated this and had saved the Pethidine against its happening, gave it now and restored peace and quiet once more, but not without several of the ladies waking up once more and demanding fresh tea.

Brown went late to her meal too, and by the time Samantha got to hers, she had no appetite for the cottage pie and two veg. kept hot on the plate and by now securely glued to it. The night cook agreed with her that it looked pretty revolting and offered egg and chips, which Samantha thankfully gobbled down with the rapidity born of the necessity of getting back to the ward, but while half of her mind was busy planning and plotting the rest of the night's work, the other half was thinking nostalgically of hot coffee and bacon and eggs and the company of Doctor ter Ossel. The telephone, shrilling at the other end of the dining room, recalled her to reality; it would be Brown.

It was, and could she come right away, please, because Mrs Jeffs had a pain in her chest and wasn't feeling at all well. Samantha crammed the rest of her supper into her mouth, and still chewing, made her way rapidly through the hospital, back to the ward. Mrs Jeffs was sitting up in bed, looking anxious, and looking almost as anxious was poor little Brown. Samantha swallowed the last of the chips, put on her bright professional smile and took Mrs Jeffs' pulse; it was racing and weak, and she was cold and clammy and a nasty colour and gasping for breath. A classic example of a pulmonary embolism—Samantha had no doubt of it.

'We'll get Doctor to take a look at you, he'll give you something for that pain in your chest,

Mrs Jeffs.' She caught Brown's eye. 'Just telephone Mr Mitchell, will you, Nurse? Ask him
if he could come—stat—and then telephone
Night Sister, please.'

She had spoken without any trace of anxi-
ety, but she frowned just a little at Brown and
hoped that Mrs Jeffs wouldn't notice. It wasn't
likely; she was a slow-thinking woman, fat—
too fat, and inclined to laziness as well as loath
to do her exercises when the physio came
round. Samantha held the frightened woman's
hand while she told her calmly that the pain
would ease and that she would feel better soon,
while with the other hand she turned on the
piped oxygen and adjusted the flow.

'Have a few breaths of air,' she offered
comfortably, and popped the mask over Mrs
Jeffs' pinched nose. She would need the heparin too—Jack would want to give it at once
and after that the morphia, because Mrs Jeffs
would need to stay very quiet for a few days,
otherwise the clot, instead of resolving, might
decide to move on somewhere else and cause
more trouble. Her mind raced ahead, although
none of her thoughts showed while she ram-

bled on in a sympathetic murmur so that presently Mrs Jeffs, finding herself still alive, took heart and calmed down, and presently when Jack Mitchell had given her the heparin and written up the morphia and Night Sister had come and gone, she went to sleep, with Brown, armed with her knitting, sitting like an anxious mother beside her bed, while Samantha led the registrar to the kitchen to warm him some coffee.

'She'll do, I fancy,' he said. 'Keep her at rest, though, she's not out of the wood yet. Will you be able to manage?'

Samantha gave him his coffee. 'Yes, of course we can—Sister will come at once if I get desperate, but while you're here, be a dear and write up something for that girl—the stab wounds—will you, just in case she wakes up again, she's so noisy. I'll get her chart.'

The rest of the night passed quietly, but they had to start early in the morning, creeping round with the bowls and the water and washing the ill patients the moment they opened their eyes. It was a relief when they could put on the lights and get the more active of the ladies out of their beds. But at least, by then, Mrs Jeffs had improved so much that Brown was able to leave her for quite long periods.

Samantha was washing Juffrouw Boot's face when she was surprised to hear her say: 'Night not good.'

'Rotten,' agreed Samantha, forgetting that her companion's English was so scanty as to be almost non-existent. 'And you've been awake, my dear, with your eyes shut so's not to bother us. Bless you.'

Juffrouw Boot's eyes stared up at her with such understanding that Samantha felt that she had understood every word. 'You really are an old dear,' she told her, and smiled a little tiredly as she turned to go.

She was astounded to find Doctor ter Ossel in the kitchen with Sir Joshua when she went to heat some milk for Juffrouw Boot. Her good morning was more in the nature of a question than a greeting, as though she didn't quite believe the evidence of her own eyes. As she put the milk to warm on the stove she said: 'I didn't think—that is, I thought you were in Birmingham.'

'So I was, dear girl, but it's less than two hours away and I didn't want to miss my breakfast.' He spoke so seriously that she wasn't sure what answer to make. Luckily the milk boiled and she was able to make good her escape and by careful planning, avoided going into the kitchen again; it would be awful if the doctor should think that she was fishing for another meal.

The report took longer than usual because she had to give Margaret exact details of Mrs Jeffs and the girl with the stab wounds. True, Sir Joshua had dried his hands and put on his jacket and been to pay both patients a visit at the unheard-of hour of seven o'clock in the morning, but as he had explained smoothly to Mrs Jeffs, the strike was forcing him to keep somewhat unusual hours. He had told Samantha that provided due care was taken, and subject to one or two instructions he wrote on their charts, he saw no immediate cause for alarm over either patient. He had commended her on her prompt action and with the same breath had enquired irritably why the devil she hadn't put out enough tea towels for his use.

Samantha hastened to apologise for this, thinking, as she did so, that probably his wife kept a dozen or so piled in her kitchen, but then she wouldn't have to wash them and boil them and get them dry by morning, all the while fighting a strong desire to get into bed and sleep the clock round.

She wished Margaret goodbye, waved to such of the patients who happened to be looking her way and made her way down the stone staircase. Brown she had sent off minutes earlier; there was no point in keeping the child hanging around while the report was being given and they had had a busy night. She had reached the last step of the last flight when Doctor ter Ossel suddenly appeared before her. 'I'll be outside the entrance, Samantha, and don't be long—I'm famished,' he told her matter-of-factly.

'But—but you don't want me to breakfast with you again?' she asked, and realized how silly that sounded.

If he found it silly too, he was kind enough not to say so. 'I should like your advice,' he went on, and she uttered after him: 'Advice?'

'That's right. About Klara—we can talk about it over breakfast.'

'Yes—well…' She hesitated, trying to frame the right words. 'You could ask it now, you don't have to take me out to a meal.'

'I don't have to do anything,' he assured her equably. 'I please myself.' Which seemed to clinch the matter.

Samantha had often heard it said that anything repeated was never as good as the first time, but if that were the case, breakfast with Doctor ter Ossel was the exception to the rule; she wasn't quite so tired for a start, and the benign waiter and the smiling attendant contrived to make her feel at ease, and over and above that, her companion, talking with an easy charm about nothing much, was gently amusing without taxing her powers of concentration too much.

She ate a hearty breakfast and it wasn't until they were having a final cup of coffee that Doctor ter Ossel remarked: 'Ah, yes, your advice, Samantha. Klara needs a new coat and presumably a hat. She will be leaving Clement's in a day or so and I feel it might be the occasion best fitted for giving them to her. A dress too, perhaps. What do you think?'

'It sounds a splendid idea. Do you know her size?'

He looked blank. 'No, that's where I thought you might help.'

'You mean measure her and so on?' She put down her cup. 'Yes, of course I will.'

'Perhaps you would be kind enough to buy them for me too?'

She nodded. 'I'll be glad to. You'll have to tell me how much you want to spend. I've got nights off in a day or two, I'll get them then.'

'Splendid—I'll pick you up outside the Home, shall I?'

She was aware of inward delight, although she said at once and a trifle coolly, 'There's no need for that, I can quite easily…'

He passed his cup and she filled it for him. 'You really are an independent miss, aren't you? I quite understand that you dislike me; you were at great pains to tell me, were you not? But it's hardly a social occasion, is it? merely a shopping expedition, done, as it were, in the line of duty.'

It became all at once imperative to explain something to him. She drew a deep breath and began, talking very fast before she could change her mind. 'I don't dislike you, not any more, really I don't. You're arrogant and off-hand and you—you laugh at me, but you've been very kind too.' She looked up from the pattern she was drawing on the tablecloth with a fork, and found him looking at her with a bright gaze which was a little disconcerting; all the same, she kept on steadily: 'You don't even work at Clement's but you've been mar-vellous in the kitchen and emptying the buck-ets and that sort of thing, and you did all that housework in the flat and ironed my uni-form...'

'Spare my blushes, dear girl, it amused me.' He paused. 'It's nice to know that this is the beginning of a beautiful friendship between us. You're free the day after tomorrow, are you not?'

Samantha was still turning over the bit about a beautiful friendship in her mind; probably he had been joking. 'Yes, I am.'

'Good. Will ten o'clock suit you? And will you come armed with Klara's vital statistics and so forth?'

She replied that yes, she would, and felt a great surge of pleasure and relief when he said: 'I meant that bit about the beautiful friendship—after all, a man never knows when he might need a good nurse.'

She laughed a little because of course he was joking, and suggested a little shyly that she might go back to the flat, and this time he didn't come in.

Although she was really very tired by now, Samantha lay awake for a little while, wondering about the doctor. He didn't seem to do much work; that he went to Holland frequently she already knew now, but why was he in London in the first place, and why was Klara with him, and why…? She fell asleep.

It was raining when she met him, a fine drizzle from a dreary grey sky, only she wasn't feeling dreary although it had been a busy night and a scramble to rush back to the flat, bath and change her clothes and eat a hasty breakfast, but she had managed it. She had been forced to wear her raincoat again, but the scarf she had draped over her hair was a gay one and gave her sleepy face the colour it lacked. She had got out her best handbag and gloves too and put on her high boots and donned the wool dress she reserved for the more special occasions in her life, not admitting to herself that she hoped that he would ask her out to lunch.

'Oxford Street?' he wanted to know as soon as she was comfortably settled beside him in the car. 'Bond Street? You decide.'

He still hadn't told her how much money she was to spend. 'I should think Marks and Spencer or Selfridges.'

'Can one not buy clothes at Fortnum and Mason's?' he asked her, and at her surprised yes, said: 'Well, let's go there first, if we don't like anything there we can always go to Harrods.'

'You didn't say how much money you wanted to spend,' she reminded him austerely, and he said at once: 'Sorry—well, I don't think Klara is quite the figure for *haute couture*, do you? but I'd like her to have something nice—' and he named a generous amount '—that's a provisional figure.'

She turned startled eyes upon him, but he was looking ahead, his powerful profile quite placid. 'That's a lot of money,' she pointed out. 'A lot of woman don't have much more than that to spend on clothes for a whole year.'

His surprise was quite genuine, she saw with amusement. Perhaps he was a rich man who didn't concern himself with such things—it was something she hadn't given much thought to, and it made her faintly uneasy. Not that she had anything against being rich, it must be a pleasant state in which to live—but did he think that she had changed her opinion of him for that reason? It was something which she would have to make clear at once, before she had time to feel awkward about it. She began: 'There's something I should like to say…' and wished she hadn't begun because she was feeling awkward already.

He gave her a brief, smiling glance. 'Do you know, dear girl, I have a suspicion that I know just what you're going to say?'

She didn't look at him. 'I daresay you do—other girls must have said it already...'

She heard him laugh. 'No, as a matter of fact, they haven't. Now, tell me if I'm wrong. You've suddenly come to the conclusion that I'm a wealthy man and at the same time you have remembered that you told me, only two days ago, that you didn't dislike me any more, and you're afraid that I might think that your change of heart is due solely to that fact. Am I right?'

'How did you know?' asked Samantha, very disconcerted.

'I am not unobservant, little Sam, and just at the moment you are wearing your feelings for all to see on your face. Besides, the very idea of you playing the role of—what do you say?—gold-digger, is ridiculous.'

She took immediate and quite illogical exception to this remark. 'You don't have to tell me,' she said vexedly. 'Gold-diggers are pretty and beautifully dressed and amusing...' She choked with rage, longing with all her heart to be just such a girl, then he might look at her. He looked at her now, with a casual glance which held mockery, as he pulled in beside a vacant parking meter, but he didn't say anything. She got out, feeling self-conscious, and marched into Fortnum and Mason's beside him, consumed with a rage she didn't understand because it wasn't against the doctor at all—it was against her ordinary face and her straight hair and not having enough money to buy the clothes she longed for.

They walked upstairs to the first floor, disdaining the lift, and began to stroll around the coat department, and Samantha, momentarily forgetful of why she was there, gazed at the garments on display, mentally choosing an outfit for herself. It was an elegant saleslady asking the doctor if his wife required anything who brought her down to earth. A little flushed in the face, she explained their wishes and became at once very businesslike and engrossed, leaving him to sit in a chair, looking quite composed and at ease, while she chose a tweed coat, suitably loose to cover his housekeeper's ample frame, and a matching, thinner tweed dress. She showed the results to the doctor, mentioned the price, which appalled her but left him quite unmoved, and asked, coldly, because she was still smarting from the nasty little smile he had given her, if he desired to purchase a hat to complete the outfit.

'Of course, dear girl. Nothing too frivolous, though—shall we inspect them together?'

They wandered round the hats, escorted by another saleslady, until he stopped at last before a feathery trifle with a pertly angled bow at one side, and said: 'Now, I like this one...'

Samantha forgot she was treating him coolly. 'Oh, no—not for your Klara.'

He turned to stare down at her, his eyes amused. 'No, not Klara,' he agreed, 'you, Sam.'

She blinked; he was making fun of her again. She didn't suppose that he meant to be unkind, perhaps he didn't realize how wretched it was to have no redeeming features at all in one's face. She thought she had got over minding that, and she was minding more than ever before. She declared with hollow gaiety: 'Oh, yes—a hat like that would suit almost anyone, but not Klara, perhaps. I thought a velvet, something not too large, but it must fit over all that hair.'

The saleslady opened a drawer and began hauling out a selection of matronly hats, and the doctor said: 'You have long hair too, Samantha.'

She edged away from him towards the growing array of hats; perhaps it would be as well for her to keep her mind on what she was doing.

'Yes, well—' she said inadequately, and picked up the first of the hats.

They had coffee afterwards, and when they had finished it her companion, quite forgetting that she hadn't been to bed yet, suggested that they might stroll around for a while. 'We might see something else for Klara,' he pointed out in such a sensible voice that she could but agree. They stowed their purchases in the Rolls' boot, and wandered off in the rain, not noticing particularly where they were going, while the doctor talked, apparently aimlessly, about himself; something he had never done before. Samantha heard with growing interest that he had an elderly grandmother of whom he was very fond, that his parents were dead, that he had two younger brothers, both in Canada, that he had a large practice which he had been forced to leave in the hands of an old friend for a short time while he dealt with business matters in London. 'A house,' he explained, 'the house where Klara had her unfortunate accident; one of my aunts was an Englishwoman and my godmother; she died recently and left her home to me and it seemed a good idea to bring Klara with me—she had never been to England and was longing to see the inside of an English house. I should have known better than to have left her alone, even for ten minutes. I blame myself very much.'

'Well, you mustn't,' declared Samantha warmly, 'for you did tell her not to touch anything until you got back. Where did you go?'

'It was all rather silly; we hadn't been in the house half an hour when I had a telephone call asking me to go to St Clement's Hospital—not your place, the one in the Midlands. A colleague of mine had been taken there after an accident and he wanted to see me. I stayed with him until he died and when I got back, hours later, it was to find Klara gone. I had told her I was going to a hospital—she remembered its name, only it was the wrong hospital.' He stopped to look down at her. 'How did you know that I told her not to touch anything?' he asked with interest. 'She speaks no English and I doubt if you have learnt much Dutch from her.'

Samantha smiled. 'It's surprising what conversations you can have, all the same,' she told him. 'I spent a good deal of time with her, you know—her hands and so forth, and she had to have everything done for her—I picked up a few words and she learnt a few from me. We understood each other very well and now we have quite long chats together.'

She wondered why he looked pleased. They had arrived on a corner of Piccadilly Circus, and she felt a little cold and shivery inside now; that was because she was tired. A sensible girl would remind him that she should go back to the flat and go to bed, but Samantha wasn't feeling sensible; she wanted to hear as much about him as possible while he was in this quiet, friendly mood; she could only suppose that he had been feeling lonely and wanted to talk about himself to someone.

She sighed without knowing it and he looked down at her again and said in the gentle voice he almost never used; 'What about lunch?' He smiled slowly. 'I...' he began again, then stopped and stared across the Circus, frowning. 'What is all that commotion over there?' he wanted to know sharply. Samantha looked too, a little put out at this interruption to the prospect of lunch. There was indeed a commotion, on the far side of the Circus, and what had been a few disjointed shouts and a handful of people waving their arms about suddenly swelled to a deafening din pierced by police whistles, while the traffic, apparently brought to a halt, snarled itself into an instant tangle. People started to run; police cars appeared from nowhere, and Samantha, standing on tiptoe and straining her eyes to see what was happening, said: 'Look, they're getting off the buses.' She caught at his arm and his hand came down on hers in instant reassurance. 'They're getting out of the taxis too,' she added, puzzled. The doctor grunted and as a small, seedy man went past them at a puffing trot, put out an arm and halted him.

'What's the matter?' he asked.

The man tried to shake off the arm. 'A bomb,' he rasped, 'over there,' he nodded behind him, 'going off any minute. Let me go!'

The doctor released him at once and used the arm to put around Samantha, who all at once was very glad of its comforting weight. 'Back the way we came,' he said without any trace of excitement, and started down Piccadilly, crossing the road at the same time. They had put perhaps a hundred yards between them and the corner, keeping to the side of the pavement and letting the stream of people race past them—a wise precaution, as it turned out, because there was a great deal of pushing and shoving and people were getting knocked down—when the world erupted behind them. Samantha would have liked to scream, but the doctor gave her no chance; he pushed her quite roughly against the wall and leaned against her, all fifteen stone of him, squeezing out her breath and shielding her completely. For a few moments she was too afraid to breathe, her head burrowed into his chest, his steady heart-beat under her cheek. She found herself auto-matically counting its beat, her trained ears noting that it was only slightly above normal while they refused to hear the fearful din going on around them. But presently she became aware of a crescendo of sound—shouts and tumbling masonry and the tinkle of glass, and far away the sing-song of ambulances or fire engines.

Her mouth, she discovered, was very dry, all the same she managed to say weakly into the thick cloth of his coat: 'Oh, dear!' aware as she said it that it was a stupid remark.

She felt his arms slacken just a little. 'You're all right, Sam? Sorry to squash you flat.' He drew away from her, still holding her, and looked her over carefully.

She guessed that she looked a perfect fright, but it didn't matter at all. 'You're all right too?' she asked him.

He nodded. 'If you feel up to it, we had better give a hand. Come along.'

He caught her hand in his and began to make a difficult way back to Piccadilly Circus. People were still running to and fro, helter-skeltering in every direction, shouting to each other, while some just stood and stared, too shocked to move. The worst of the damage was on the other side of Eros, close to the statue, but the blast had smashed every pane of glass in the neighbourhood. They walked past the ruined windows of various shops and edged their way through the stationary traffic round the statue, then crossed the road towards Coventry Street. Here the havoc was the greatest, yet not as bad as it might have been, for while the big buildings around had lost their windows and chunks of their walls, they still stood. But there were a number of damaged cars and a bus, blown over on to its side. It was here that the doctor stopped, for it was obvious that it had been full at the time of the explosion and none of its passengers had had the time to get away. There were police already there, freeing the people as quickly as they were able, and Doctor ter Ossel wasted no time in tapping one burly officer on the shoulder.

'This young lady is a nurse and I am a doctor. Can we be of help?'

The man nodded his head at the half dozen or so victims already sitting or lying on the road, and went on with his task of easing an elderly lady out of a too-small window. Doctor ter Ossel gave Samantha's hand a tug. 'Come on,' he said crisply, just as though, she thought wearily, she wasn't showing willing. There were a great many injured lying around, now she had time to look. After a time she lost count of the rough bandages she had applied, the broken arms and legs she had steadied while the doctor splinted them in a makeshift fashion, the cut heads and faces she had done her best to clean. The ambulances began to arrive very shortly, but they had to make their way through the traffic still being unravelled by the police. Samantha had no idea what the time was when at length the doctor observed: 'There—they don't need us any more—there are plenty of ambulances and hospital teams now. We'll go.' All she knew was that she ached all over and her eyes felt hot and prickly in her head. She got up off her knees where she had been holding a small boy steady while the doctor slid a dislocated shoulder back into its socket, watched the child borne away by an ambulance man, and then took her companion's hand like a child as he started to pick his way through the rubble. It seemed a great distance to where the car was parked, but perhaps that was a good thing, she thought sleepily, for it was quite undamaged. He settled her into it and got in beside her.

'We were going to have lunch,' he sounded rueful, 'but now I think you should go home to bed.'

Samantha agreed quietly. He was right, of course; she was dog-tired, but she was also very hungry; she would have to make a pot of tea at the flat and eat some biscuits. She glanced surreptitiously at her watch and saw that it was almost two o'clock, a fact which surprised her, for it seemed the morning had merged into afternoon while they had been busy in what to her had been a matter of minutes.

It took some time to reach the flat, for they had to make a wide detour. They spoke very little on the journey and as he at last stopped the car before the flat, she roused herself to fumble at her safety belt. He undid it for her, said 'Stay there,' and got out to knock on Mr Cockburn's window. Whatever it was he said took only a few moments, then he came back to open her door and help her out. He kept an arm round her as they went up the steps, too, something she was glad of, for her legs felt unexpectedly wobbly.

At the flat door he took her handbag from her, extracted the key and opened the door, pushing her gently before him into the little hall.

'I shall be ten minutes,' he said with calm authority. 'When I get back you are to be undressed and in bed, is that clear? And those are doctor's orders.'

Samantha nodded her head meekly, feeling far too tired to argue about something she had been longing to do for the last couple of hours. When he had gone, she undressed slowly, putting everything away even more neatly than was her custom. She had just got into bed when she heard him return. He went straight to the kitchen, and presently she heard the kettle being filled at the sink and the faint clash of saucepans on the stove. He seemed destined to housekeep for her, she thought drowsily, and closed her eyes.

'No, you don't,' said the doctor briskly. 'Drink this first.'

It was tea, a mug full, nicely strong and milky and sweet. She sipped it slowly and had barely finished it when he came back again, this time with a soup bowl and a spoon. 'This too,' he ordered firmly.

The soup was delicious. She spooned it up and decided that she had never tasted anything like it before. She said so when Doctor ter Ossel appeared in the doorway once more.

'I'm not surprised,' he said laconically, 'I laced it with brandy.'

She looked at him with owl's eyes. 'Brandy? We haven't any…'

'No, but I have.' He took the bowl from her and sat down on the side of the bed and took her pulse, studying her face with a doctor's eyes. 'That's better, you look more like the indomitable Staff Nurse Fielding once more. Not,' he added, 'that I found you unattractive as a terrified, whey-faced half-asleep girl, working like a Trojan in the middle of a very nasty mess.' He bent and kissed her gently. 'I like you with your hair around your shoulders,' he observed. 'And now go to sleep.'

Her eyes closed as she heard the click of the closing door. She didn't wake at all, not even when her three friends, at first singly, and then all three together, came to see how she was. When they saw that nothing would rouse her, they went back to the sitting room to gaze, once again, at a bottle of three-star brandy, several tins of expensive soup, a cooked chicken, and a quantity of apples and oranges and grapes spilling out of their bag—gifts from heaven, presumably.

The doctor called the next morning, while Samantha was still mooning round the flat, try-ing to make up her mind to get dressed. He eyed her carefully and then said: 'I thought I had better come and see how you were. I feel responsible for yesterday's fracas—you wouldn't have been anywhere near there if I hadn't asked you...'

She didn't much care for this remark, for it seemed as though he considered it unlikely for her to shop at the more fashionable stores, but she could hardly say so, indeed she had to thank him for his care of her. She did so, a little haltingly.

His grey eyes bored into hers. 'You called me Giles, do you remember?'

She nodded; she remembered very well. 'Yes, well—it was all so unexpected. I—I wasn't thinking.'

'What a pity,' he commented. 'I hoped that you meant it. Could you not, now that we are friends, remember to call me by my first name?'

She nodded again, and before she could speak, he mentioned casually that he was returning to Holland on the following day.

'Going away?' said Samantha. 'And what about Juffrouw Boot? Is she going too? Have you finished your business in London—aren't you coming back?'

He took quite a long time to answer and even when he did it wasn't very satisfactory. 'I live in Holland and I work there—most of the time, at least, and as for the business matters—these things take time. I find I have to wait; the other party concerned isn't quite of my mind.' He opened his eyes wide and stared at her hard. 'Given time, they'll come round to my way of thinking.' He smiled slowly as he spoke.

She had no idea what he was talking about; besides, disappointment had reduced her powers of speech to nil. This will teach you, my girl, she admonished herself as she looked at him, trying to think of something to say. It was as though she were seeing him for the first time and she loved what she saw. The knowledge hit her like a blow because it was so unexpected, and she swallowed back the great surge of feeling racing over her. 'Well, I hope it will be satisfactory for you,' she said in a stilted voice. 'You'll forgive me if I ask you to go now. I've got—got things to do.' She put out a hand which shook ever so slightly, and had it engulfed in his. 'Goodbye, Doctor ter Ossel.'

'Giles.'

'Giles.' She made herself smile as she went to the door with him, and when he had gone, stood leaning against it, listening to his quick tread on the stairs. When she could no longer hear them she went back to her room and got dressed, sobbing her heart out as she did so.

CHAPTER FOUR

A WEEK LATER the strike was over and Samantha had come—unexpectedly—off night duty. She had visited Juffrouw Boot during her nights off, hoping uselessly that Giles ter Ossel might be there too, but he wasn't. She admired the coat and dress they had chosen and arranged the hat on the old lady's severely pinned-back hair, and Juffrouw Boot had smiled and caught her hand in her own, bulky with its dressings still. She was going the next day, Samantha was able to make out, but whether she was returning to Holland or remaining in London it was impossible to tell. Anyway, Samantha had thought, what did it matter—the whole episode was finished with and the quicker she made up her mind to that, the better. She had fancied herself in love on numerous occasions, but she knew now that it hadn't been love at all. She only hoped that she would be able to forget Giles very quickly, although she was doubtful of this; it seemed worse because she hadn't liked him at first. She kissed Juffrouw Boot goodbye on her leathery cheek, wishing her well in a cheerful voice, and went back to the flat where she spent the rest of the day doing a great deal of quite unnecessary cleaning, thankful that she had something to do to pass the endless day.

She had been transferred to Private Patients' Wing when she came off night duty, something which she detested—for one thing there was a great deal of extra work because the patients, naturally enough, had their own rooms, and over and above that, tended to ring the bell for the slightest thing, and took umbrage unless they received attention at once. The one ray of cheer for Samantha was that it was to be only a temporary posting; a couple of weeks at the outside, Miss Fletcher, the number eight, had told her, and then she was to be offered the post of Junior Night Sister on the surgical side, should she care to apply for it. She didn't like night duty, but a Sister, even a junior one, earned a better salary than a staff nurse; she would be able to go to Langton Herring far more often, besides being able to help her grandparents to a far greater extent than she could now. She knew that she should feel pleased and excited about it, but she didn't; her mind was still full of Giles, and nothing else mattered very much.

She reported for day duty at five o'clock in the evening, because, following hospital custom, having come off night duty that morning, she was considered sufficiently rested to report for day duty that same day in the late afternoon—an erroneous idea which someone, a long time ago, must have thought up. Samantha, dragging her feet up the stairs leading to the new wing, silently railed at the unknown instigator of the idea. She was a few minutes early; a good thing, for Private Wards Sister, Perkins by name, was a great disciplinarian. She was also a silent woman, giving her reports in a kind of verbal shorthand and never using two words when one would do, she was waiting in her office now, making sure that Samantha would arrive on time. She took her eyes off the clock on the wall before her, bade Samantha seat herself, and plunged at once into the report. Twelve patients, she began crisply and proceeded to give details of them and when she had finished:

'A case this evening, Staff Nurse. In number ten, under your care. Staff Nurse Manners will do treatments and write the report until you are familiar with the patients. Acute infective hepatitis—quite poorly. Doctor Duggan—Doctor Duggan was a consultant in the hospital as well as being on its board of governors—is the personal doctor of the family with whom she is staying.' She got up. 'Right, Staff Nurse. We'll let you know your off duty tomorrow.'

Samantha murmured politely, got herself out of the little room and closed the door quietly. Old Perky had been quite chatty for once. She went to find Manners next who greeted her with a: 'There you are, ducky, and am I glad to see you—we've got the most ghastly bunch of PPs you ever set eyes on, lying back amongst their hot-house flowers and their champagne bottles and After Eight Mints, and not one of them ill—at least, not so's you'd notice.' She thumped up the pillows of the bed she was preparing for the new case. 'I daresay this one will be as bad—I wish you luck, Sam.' She cast a glance at her friend. 'You look a bit peaked—night duty too much for you?'

Samantha said no and went to the other side of the bed to help.

'What's this the grapevine's passing around that you're to get the Junior Night Sister's job on Surgical? All set for a career, my girl, aren't you?'

'Well, no—not really, Liz. I don't particularly want to stay for the rest of my life...'

Her friend gave her no chance to finish her sentence. 'Get married like me. Another month or two and I'll be saying bye-bye to this place.'

She looked complacently at Samantha, as well she might; she was a pretty girl and her father was a doctor; she had had no difficulty in meeting a number of young men bent on making their names in the same profession. Samantha, while not envious, wished that she had had Liz's opportunities as well as her pretty face, and changed the conversation.

'I wonder why I came off night duty? I'm not due off for another two or three weeks, you know. You're not short-staffed, are you?'

Liz shrugged her shoulders. 'No more than usual. But I do wonder why old Perkins told you to take over this case—she was supposed to come in two days ago—I suppose there was some hitch. I'm going to take the report from old Perky now—the moment she's gone we'll have a cup of coffee before I go to supper. If you feel you can, you could start the evening temps.'

The new patient was admitted while Liz was in the dining room, and Samantha, having wrestled with the suppers, was dutifully going round from one patient to the next, enquiring if the meal had been enjoyed. She had got as far as the appendix in room three, who, from the way in which she was carrying on, one would suppose had suffered the removal of her entire inside, when a student nurse edged her way in to say that the new case was on the way up—a sufficiently good reason for Samantha to abandon her round and whisk to the end room along the corridor.

The case was a girl, young and golden-haired, and even with the yellow complexion her illness had inflicted upon her, very pretty. Samantha tucked her up in bed with unhurried sympathy and a cheerful face, begged her to lie quiet for a moment while she got her particulars, and went to find whoever had come in with her. An elderly woman, grey-haired and still attractive, who introduced herself as Mrs Devenish.

'I'm no relation,' she told Samantha. 'Antonia was staying with me for a week or two and became ill, and Doctor Duggan thought it best for her to come into hospital for a little while. Clement's is miles away from where I live, but he's on the consulting staff here, isn't he?'

Samantha said that yes, he was and offered a chair before seating herself at Sister's desk. 'A few particulars…?' she invited.

She was given them briskly, without the usual humming and haaing and getting the age right and did it matter if some really fresh eggs were left for the patient's breakfast and what about the laundry? There was a refreshing absence of these questions. She was told that the girl's name was Antonia van Duyren, that she was eighteen, that she was Dutch and lived at a town called Dokkum in Friesland with her mother.

'Her brother is my son-in-law,' explained Mrs Devenish. 'I've telephoned him and I daresay that he and Sappha—my daughter—will be over as soon as he can get away from the practice. You'll want my telephone number, I expect.'

And when Samantha had written it all down in her rather large, clear writing, Mrs Devenish asked if she might go back to the patient's room and unpack her things. 'I know you're busy—nurses always are—may I come and see her tomorrow, do you suppose?'

'Of course, Mrs Devenish.' Samantha had taken to the cheerful, understanding lady. 'Private patients may have visitors when they like, you know. She looks a bit low, but I daresay she'll love to see you in the morning.'

Presently Samantha went along to room ten, to find Mrs Devenish gone and her patient in tears. 'What's up?' enquired Samantha sympathetically as she shook down the thermometer.

'I look such a fright,' said the girl in excellent English.

Samantha considered her. 'Well, you're so pretty you can get away with it,' she said encouragingly, 'and it won't last long. I'm going to wash your face and hands, and presently the registrar will be along to see you—he's rather a sweetie.'

The girl brightened. 'Is he? won't he mind…?'

Samantha shook her neat head. 'He wouldn't notice a slight tinge of yellow. Doctor Duggan's coming in too.' She busied herself with a bowl of water and towels and presently said: 'There, isn't that better? I'm going to comb your hair and arrange you nicely on your pillows, and if you feel irritable don't mind me—it's all part and parcel of your illness and it won't matter in the least.'

The girl smiled. 'You're nice,' she pronounced. 'What is your name?'

'Staff Nurse Fielding.'

The girl frowned. 'No, I mean your name…'

'Oh—Samantha.'

'May I call you that? And you shall call me Tonia.'

'Why not?' agreed Samantha, who had taken a liking to her patient. 'Only for heaven's sake call me Staff when Sister's here—she's a bit straight-laced.'

Tonia frowned. 'Laced?' she hazarded. 'Corsets, perhaps?'

Samantha giggled. 'I've no doubt, but it really means she's a bit strict.'

'And you? You are not strict—you are like my dear Sappha, my brother's wife. He adores her, for she is beautiful.'

'That would be a help,' murmured Samantha, and thought of Giles as she tidied the bed.

John Wells, the Medical Registrar, came next, followed almost immediately by Doctor Duggan, who talked gently, wrote a great deal in his fine copperplate handwriting on his patient's chart, told her it might be better if she didn't look at herself in the mirror for a day or two, and parted, escorted very properly by Samantha, to the entrance of the PP wing.

At the big swing doors he paused to look at her and say: 'Thank you, Staff Nurse. What is this rumour I hear that you are to become Junior Night Sister on Surgical?'

How news got around! 'Well,' she began, 'I don't know about that, sir. I haven't been offered the post yet, only told that I may apply for it if I wished to.'

'Ah, yes—just so. And you intend to do this?'

She just stopped herself from shrugging her shoulders. 'I suppose I shall, sir.'

He prepared to leave. 'Well, I hope that you will consider well before you decide—there are always alternatives.'

He trod with suitable dignity down the stairs, leaving her gaping after him. What on earth had he meant? Didn't he want her to have the job? As far as she knew he didn't dislike her, so why in heaven's name was he giving her such peculiar advice? Samantha frowned, deep in thought as she went back down the corridor to number ten, and encountered John Wells on the way, for he, naturally enough, had stayed behind on some excuse or other in

order to have a few words with his new patient. He stopped as they reached each other
and said: 'Hullo, Sam. What's this I hear about
you being offered this job...'

Samantha fought back a strong feeling of
revulsion at the idea of being a Night Sister,
especially as everyone she met seemed to think
that she would jump at the chance—almost as
though they realized that her chances of getting
married were so slender that it was imperative
that she should carve a career for herself. But
although her common sense told her that this
was a splendid opportunity to start up the lad-
der of the nursing profession, her heart begged
her not to do it, for the simple and ridiculous
reason that she might one day meet Giles ter
Ossel again, and if he thought she was a career
girl, what little interest he had in her might
disappear entirely. And what good would that
do you? asked common sense; her heart's un-
spoken wish that he might fall in love with her
was so ludicrous that she stifled the very idea
mercilessly and said quite snappily. 'John, for
goodness' sake—I haven't been offered the job
yet and everyone's taking it for granted...'

He gave her a concerned, faintly reproving look. 'You need more sleep, Sam old girl,' he observed kindly, and then: 'That's a pretty creature in room ten. I'll pop back later and make sure she'll be all right for the night.' He slapped her in a brotherly fashion and went on his way whistling, leaving Samantha, usually mild-tempered, decidedly put out.

Antonia was ill—not desperately so, but bad enough to be sorry for herself and remarkably irritable with those who happened to be around her, although during her more comfortable moments, she apologised very prettily for making such a nuisance of herself. Samantha found her a handful, but she liked her too, and compared with Captain Trent, RN retired, in room nine, a fiery old gentleman who conducted life as though he were still on the bridge, and Miss Winifred Good, who occupied number eight, called everyone darling and was always ringing her bell for someone to put her hair in curlers, Antonia was infinitely preferable. They got on well together, even on the days when Antonia was feeling low and snapping at everyone, including Samantha, who took no notice at all; Antonia was, after all, quite ill; her jaundice was severe and she had considerable fever from time to time.

It was on the third day, just after a light lunch which Antonia had not wished to eat and which Samantha had coaxed her to try, when there was a knock on the door. Samantha hurriedly finished, arranged her patient's hair to its greatest advantage and, with a glance at the girl in the bed, begged whoever it was to come in.

Two people entered; a strikingly pretty girl with curling hair and the kind of nose Samantha had always longed for, wrapped in a fur-lined tweed coat, and a youngish, dark man with flyaway eyebrows which dominated his dark good looks and gave him a slightly satyrish look. He was very tall as well as being large and it was very obvious to Samantha that the young lady with him was the apple of his eye.

'Is it all right if we come in?' began the girl, to be interrupted by Antonia's excited voice. 'Sappha—Rolf, oh, how lovely to see you! What a gorgeous surprise!' She sat up in bed and flung herself at them both, and the girl said gently, 'Tonia, my poor poppet—do you feel very wretched? However did you come to catch it?'

Her brother was eyeing her with mock horror. 'Yellow as a guinea,' he remarked, and turned to Samantha. 'How do you do? It is Staff Nurse Fielding, I think? My...' he paused, then went on smoothly, 'mother-in-law told us about you. This is my wife, Sappha. You have already met Mrs Devenish, of course.' He smiled and became instantly charming. 'Is Tonia a great trial? I'm afraid she has been rather spoilt.'

Samantha made a suitable reply and went on to say that yes, she had met Mrs Devenish and that lady had visited regularly. Antonia was getting on nicely, she added.

Tonia's brother nodded. 'Good—as soon as it's practicable, we'll get her home, for after the acute stage she will only be blocking a bed.' A remark which called forth a soft murmur of protest from his wife and a decidedly sharp one from the invalid.

'But I'm ill,' declared his sister. 'Most of the time I feel awful.' She appealed to Samantha. 'Don't I, Samantha?'

'Yes, of course you're ill, Tonia, but you're getting better all the time—it won't last for ever, you know.'

'But there'll be no one to look after me,' declared the bed's occupant woefully. 'Sappha's got baby Rolf and Mother can't...'

Her brother's dark gaze rested for the fraction of a second on the unconscious Samantha. 'We'll attend to that when the time comes. We're going now, but we'll be back in the evening.' He went to the door and opened it and returned with an armful of books and magazines and a large quantity of flowers. 'We almost forgot these, Tonia.' He put them on the end of the bed, embraced his sister and waited patiently while his wife took a somewhat longer farewell of the patient.

'We may come back late?' he asked Samantha. 'Is there any particular time when it's easier for you?'

She considered. 'I don't think so, thank you. We make beds and so on between half past five and half past six, and it's supper at seven. I'm off duty at five o'clock, but I'll let Staff Nurse Manners know—but come when you like, we can always change the work routine a bit.'

They took their leave of her and went away, a striking pair and supremely happy—she didn't need Tonia to tell her that when they had gone. It would be nice to be married to a man like that, mused Samantha, collecting the flowers to arrange, someone who didn't say very much but who would always be there, loving you. Giles, for instance. She sighed and Antonia asked: 'Are you tired? You look sad.'

Samantha's reply was such a vigorous denial that she almost convinced herself.

She went on duty the next morning with her mind almost made up to apply for the Sister's post. She had written and told her grandparents about it and hadn't mentioned Doctor ter Ossel at all, although her grandmother had asked several questions about him in her letters. A very small piece of her mind was still protesting against common sense, though, and she knew that the smallest happening would be sufficient for her to use it as an excuse and to send common sense flying.

And Antonia was difficult; Samantha had wished her good morning when she had gone on duty and then departed to attend to the manifold wants of Captain Trent and Miss Good, supervise the giving of breakfast trays, take the report and then give out the medicines required and generally have the wing on its feet by the time Sister Perkins came on duty, so that by the time she got back to the Dutch girl, it was considerably after nine o'clock, and Antonia, never at her best in the morning, was in a very bad temper indeed.

'I am tired,' she declared in her accented English, 'of these other nurses. I wish only you to look after me, Sam. Rolf must arrange it.'

Samantha was gathering together the necessities for a bed-bath, because Antonia had a temperature again and would have to stay in bed until it had gone down. 'You'll be lucky,' she said vulgarly. 'We're short-staffed as it is and there are other patients here, you know.' She advanced to the bed. 'Come on, cheer up, Tonia, you're getting better, you know. Why don't you wear that gorgeous nightie Mrs van Duyren brought you and I'll tie your hair back with a ribbon, then you can sit back and look through those magazines and then lend them to me.'

'You like clothes?' instantly diverted, Antonia wanted to know.

'Well, I don't wear uniform all round the clock, you know. I adore clothes.'

They spent a pleasant half hour after that, interspersing the dull business of bed-bathing with quick glimpses of *Vogue*'s and *Harper & Queen*'s pages. The fact that the Dutch girl was quite unshattered by the prices of the various garments pictured therein, while Samantha was secretly horrified, made no difference. Antonia, with Samantha's enthusiastic help, chose for herself a large quantity of clothes which she was confident her brother would be delighted to buy her. 'He buys Sappha heaps of things—he never stops. He's very rich,' she added, 'and he's a baron, so Sappha isn't a missus, she's a baroness.'

Samantha received these confidences with calm, for the two people in question would be nice whatever they were and without a cent to their name; some people couldn't be spoilt. Giles, for instance; she hadn't meant to think of him, but he was always there, at the back of her head, well battened down, and now he had popped up once more. He was like that too, she was sure—one of the world's fortunate ones who at the same time hadn't allowed himself to be spoilt by good fortune. She sighed, thinking of him, and Antonia said at once: 'You are unhappy—you were yesterday, too. I shall buy you a present, dear Sam—that beautiful hat like a cartwheel on the cover of *Harper*'s.'

'What a dear you are,' said Samantha impulsively, tidying the room as she talked, 'but I'd never wear it, you know.' She gave a soft gurgle of laughter. 'I could wear it on duty, of course.'

Antonia, her depressed spirits once more elevated, laughed too, they were giggling together when there was a knock on the door and one of the student nurses put her head in. 'There's a visitor,' she said.

'OK,' said Samantha, 'we're now open to the public.'

She was at the foot of the bed, pulling its counterpane straight, her back to the door and at Antonia's happy shriek of 'Giles!' she became quite motionless, feeling the blood drain away from her face and the frantic hammering of her heart, speechless with joy at a coincidence which happened only in romantic novels, but the joy was short-lived—she might have guessed that a lovely girl like Antonia would have known him already and charmed him for ever. She wished that she was anywhere else but where she was at that moment, standing there like an idiot, unable to move, watching her patient's face alight with her feelings. But wishing wouldn't help, so she turned round to meet his pleasant: 'Hullo, Samantha,' as he strode towards the bed, to envelop Antonia in a gentle hug. And Antonia put up her face to kiss him; Samantha, suddenly very busy, snatched up the clean towels she had just arranged so neatly, and made for the door. 'The laundry,' she said by way of explanation, although she was sure that neither of them either heard or cared.

In the corridors she snarled at one of the student nurses, flung the towels pettishly into the linen room, and was on the point of doing quite unnecessary battle with an inoffensive ward maid when Sister Perkins came into view, uttered: 'Coffee, Staff,' and disappeared again. Such a summons, whatever Samantha's feelings, was not to be ignored; the staff nurse on duty enjoyed the doubtful privilege of drinking her elevenses with Sister Perkins.

She had almost finished her coffee when the nurse whose head she had just bitten off put it cautiously round the door. 'Excuse me, Sister, but Staff's wanted in room ten.'

Sister Perkins glanced at Samantha's almost empty cup. 'Go,' she ordered briefly, and Samantha, with the greatest possible reluctance, went.

Giles ter Ossel was still there, of course, large and disturbing and, she saw with rising annoyance, looking amused. She was barely through the door when Antonia shrilled: 'Sam, you never told me that you knew Giles.'

'I've only met him,' said Samantha dampeningly, dismissing breakfasts together, a morning's shopping, bomb outrage, tulips and daffodils, and the ironing of her uniform in one reckless gesture, 'and why should I have told you when I didn't know that you knew the doctor?'

Antonia digested this muddled sentence and said coaxingly: 'You sound cross—were you doing something important?'

'I was having my coffee.'

'Well, you can blame Giles—he suggested I sent for you.'

Samantha heard him chuckle. 'Antonia, my dearest girl, don't say another word. I think I am not in Samantha's good books.'

'Don't be absurd,' protested Samantha, very haughty. 'I haven't given you a thought. Why did you want me?' she addressed Antonia pointedly, turning a shoulder to the doctor.

'Only to ask when Giles can come and visit me,' answered Antonia airily. 'I mean, he's deeply involved with me—like family, you understand, therefore he wishes to see me as often as he may.'

'Well, not before ten in the morning, and it's best for you to have a rest between one and two o'clock each day, otherwise there's all the rest of the day.' She frowned, a little puzzled, for surely Antonia knew all this already? Each patient was given a little card with such information upon it; besides, Giles had visited Juffrouw Boot, so he must have known. It reminded her to ask: 'How is Juffrouw Boot?'

She had addressed his waistcoat and didn't raise her eyes as he answered: 'Very well—she sends her love to you. She wanted to come with me this time, but she must wait a little longer, though I desperately need a woman's advice about the house.' He spoke blandly and when she darted a look at his face, he gave her a casual smile, so she said, equally casual: 'Indeed?' and turned to go.

'I suppose you wouldn't be so kind as to give me some more advice?' His voice was so meek that she turned round to look at him uncertainly. 'Advice?'

'Yes, the house this time. I know nothing of sheets and blankets and so forth—Klara was going to see to all that. I suppose you couldn't spare the time…?'

Samantha had her mouth open to say no, but Antonia was a little quicker.

'Of course she will, won't you, dear Sam—she is so kind and willing, Giles. If I were well enough I would love to help you, but as I am not Samantha shall do it for me instead.' She turned her eyes, very blue in her still yellow face, upon Samantha, who put on what she hoped was a non-committal expression. 'I hardly think…' she began, and had the thread of her speech snapped off by the doctor's hearty: 'You're too modest, Samantha, I'm sure you will know just what to buy. When are you free?'

Again Antonia spoke up. 'She's got a day off tomorrow, haven't you, Sam—and I don't in the least mind her going with you.'

Samantha tried not to see the smile he gave the Dutch girl. 'I have several things I wish to do,' she told him.

'What, for instance?' His voice was silky.

'Well…'

'You aren't breaking a date or anything like that?'

'No.' She was sorry the moment she had said it; she should have said yes.

'Then that's settled. Would eleven o'clock be too early for you?'

'You'll come and see me first?' Antonia demanded.

'Naturally—I'll be in this evening too.'

'Then give me a kiss, dear Giles, and go away, because Samantha has to force me to take my nourishment now and I may get a little cross.'

He laughed at that and bent to hug her again, said goodbye to Samantha in the lightest of tones, and went away. When he had gone, and for the rest of the day, she was forced to listen to Antonia's almost ceaseless talk of him; she had known him almost all her life, she assured Samantha earnestly, and besides, he was a great and lifelong friend of Rolf's, which was a good thing, his youngest sister pointed out, for he was very old-fashioned and strict in his views and would not allow her to have boyfriends he didn't approve of. None of these items of news, interesting though they were, cheered Samantha in the slightest. She had been surprised and happy to see Giles again, but that feeling hadn't lasted—indeed, she told herself gloomily, it would have been better if they had not met again; if only she hadn't been posted to PP in this quite unnecessary fashion, if only he hadn't returned to England again, if only he hadn't been a close friend of Antonia's family and someone even closer to Antonia. Samantha shied away from useless regrets and drew comfort from the fact that she would be seeing him the next day, but when she reflected upon this, there wasn't much comfort there; for as far as she could see she had been invited for no other reason than to make herself useful. It was a pity that she hadn't refused out of hand, but somehow Giles seemed to get his own way once he had made up his mind.

She was quite glad to find it pouring with rain when she got up the next morning, for perversely, she was determined to make no effort to improve her appearance. Accordingly she went down to the Home entrance clad in her mackintosh again and wearing a headscarf tied severely under her firm little chin; at least the doctor would know that she wasn't angling for a free lunch.

He greeted her with a casual hullo, stowed her in the car, got in beside her and drove off without further talk, so that Samantha felt forced, after a few minutes' silence, to chat. She touched upon Antonia, the awfulness of the weather, the busyness of the streets, and finally asked to which shop they were going.

'Oh, we will go to my house first,' he told her. 'Rolf and Sappha should be there by now.'

'Then why do you want me?' she cried. 'The—the baroness could advise you.'

'So she could, but she particularly asked that you should come.'

It was on the tip of Samantha's tongue to ask why, but she seemed to be asking a lot of questions and not getting very satisfactory answers. She sat silent while he took the car through Knightsbridge, to turn off presently into a quiet street, lined with tall houses. But at its end, where it ended in a high wall and a narrow mews entrance, there was a smaller house, one storey high and of a miniature elegance which took her fancy immediately, and when the doctor stopped before its freshly painted door, she was quite delighted. 'Oh, is this it?' she wanted to know.

Her companion assured her that it was. 'A bijou residence, I believe it is called, and a little on the small side for me, but since I own it I might as well make use of it.'

'I should think so!' said Samantha indignantly. 'Why, it's quite beautiful.'

'Come inside, then.'

The hall was certainly very small and seemed smaller because of the doctor's size, but the sitting room was large enough and most comfortably furnished. Antonia's brother and his wife were sitting in it and got up to meet them. 'Hullo,' said Sappha cheerfully. 'I'll go and get the coffee now you're here and then we can plunge into the linen cupboard. You are a dear to come on your day off, but neither of these men are of the least help… May I show Samantha the kitchen, Giles?'

The kitchen was small but planned by a genius. Samantha, looking round her, could think of nothing which she would want to alter. The natural-coloured wooden table and chairs, the brown-tiled floor, the straw-coloured wallpaper and the dresser filled with blue china—they all made a perfect whole. There was even the tiniest of paved yards outside the back door too, with small tubs filled with bulbs and one or two small trees.

'Nice, isn't it?' asked Sappha, arranging blue mugs on a tray. 'I believe Giles is rather enjoying himself planning it all, though it's a dreadful waste until he marries.'

Samantha absorbed this information without pleasure. 'Will he live in England, then?' she wanted to know.

'Lord, no,' said Sappha, pouring cream into a jug. 'He's got a huge practice in Haarlem, you know—lots of consultant work and a medical finger in a great many pies there. He comes over here quite a bit, though. This will make a dear little home from home. Will you bring the biscuits?'

They talked of nothing in particular while they drank their coffee and presently the girls went up the narrow circular staircase at the back of the hall and inspected the two large bedrooms and one small one which led from the microscopic landing. They were furnished with the same eye for colour as the rooms downstairs, as were the two small bathrooms.

'Doctor ter Ossel's godmother must have had exquisite taste,' commented Samantha, only to be told that before Giles had started on the place it had been pure Art Nouveau: 'Lots of Favrile glass and stained glass lampshades and water lilies, quite hideous. There was a nice little settee, though, and one or two things Giles kept.'

'Oh—did he plan all this—' Samantha waved a small capable hand in all directions— 'himself?'

Sappha nodded. 'Isn't it funny how doctors and surgeons have an artistic streak? Have you noticed? They play the violin or paint or have an eye for interior decorating.'

'Does—does your husband paint?'

'He plays the piano very well. I didn't discover that until after we were married.' Sappha smiled a little and went on in a more businesslike voice: 'Let's decide now—about towels, do you think chocolate brown to match the wall tiles and then white ones to match the paintwork? and perhaps a sharp contrast...'

'Marmalade and lime green,' suggested Samantha, and was a little surprised when Sappha agreed at once. 'Good—now sheets and things. Do you like coloured ones? No? Nor do I. White, then—they'll have to be linen because Giles is fussy—and hemstitched, don't you think? Blankets—well, they'll be easy; pink for this room, don't you think, and blue in the second bedroom, that leaves the small room...'

'With all that lovely Chippendale,' said Samantha, 'pale buttercup would look nice.'

Sappha nodded her lovely head. 'It would—let's go and tell Giles.'

'Doesn't he want a say in the matter at all?' enquired Samantha.

Her companion laughed. 'Not he—he likes poking round for furniture and so on, but he opted out of this part of it.'

'Yes,' persisted Samantha, 'but supposing he marries and his wife doesn't like any of the things we've chosen?'

'I think she will—if not, he'll give it all away and tell her to go and get what she wants.'

Samantha's careful soul was revolted. 'But that's extravagant,' she protested.

'Wildly.' And Sappha led the way downstairs.

The men were sitting where they had left them, wreathed in smoke, puffing gently at their pipes and discussing malnutrition in the elderly. Giles received their advice with equanimity, thanked them for their efforts on his behalf and proposed that they should go somewhere for lunch—a proposal received with instant approbation by Sappha and her husband and mixed feelings by Samantha. Giles was far too well-mannered to do other than include her in his invitation while not particularly wishing her to accept. She declined nicely but firmly while not quite meeting his eye, and as she stood up said, with what she hoped was suitable nonchalance: 'I've some shopping I simply must do.'

'Rubbish,' declared Giles, and added silkily, 'unless you simply can't stand our company any longer?'

Samantha's normally mild nature came to the boil at that; there was nothing worse, she discovered at that moment, than to make a gesture which involved some sort of sacrifice to oneself, and then to have it tossed back at one, especially when the tosser was smiling in such an annoying fashion.

'Don't be ridiculous,' she begged him in a scathing voice which unfortunately carried the hint of a wobble. 'You're just trying to annoy me.'

The thick eyebrows rose. 'But of course I am, for if I can get you cross enough, you'll say yes.'

He smiled, and without in the least meaning to do so, she smiled back at him, and he nodded his head and went on: 'There's a place in Sloane Street—Carlton Tower, isn't it? Let's go there.'

They ate beef bourguignonne, followed by strawberries Romanoff, and Samantha found time between the lighthearted talk to wonder where one obtained strawberries in February, and then, rendered a little uncaring by reason of the excellent claret she had been drinking, gobbled them up delicately. It was over coffee, during a pause in the conversation, that Rolf van Duyren leaned across the table to tell her that Antonia would be going home quite soon. 'You'll come back with her, won't you, Samantha?' he asked.

CHAPTER FIVE

SAMANTHA, about to drink her coffee, put the cup down again very carefully, staring at the Baron. She felt like a rabbit under the hypnotic eye of a snake, save that the Baron's dark eye was kindly, even if compelling, and she, unlike the rabbit, felt no fear, only a sudden explosion of excitement somewhere under her ribs.

'Tonia's a handful,' went on her brother in a matter-of-fact voice, 'and my mother isn't strong, and let me be honest—my little sister, being the youngest in the family, is spoilt. She and my mother live near us in Dokkum, but Sappha—' he flung a lightning, loving look at his wife, 'has our son to look after. Tonia likes you too, which means that she will do as you wish in a slavish fashion which I hope won't pall on you too much.' He smiled as he finished speaking and Samantha, looking at him, could quite understand why Sappha looked so radiantly happy; he was almost as nice a man as Giles.

'It would only be for a week or two,' murmured the Baron with deceptive humbleness.

Sappha hadn't spoken, although she was smiling a little and looking hopeful, and Giles—Giles was sitting back in his chair, looking at the far wall in a detached way, as though the conversation had no interest for him whatsoever. Samantha felt a flicker of disappointment and knew that she was being unreasonable; why should he be interested? But she was mistaken, though, for he transferred his gaze to her face.

'Tonia may be spoilt,' he conceded, 'but she's a very dear girl. There is no earthly reason why you should disrupt your career, even for a couple of weeks, but I know that all three of us would be everlastingly grateful if you did.' He smiled a little and Samantha thought that he put the Baron quite in the shade as he went on: 'Doctor Duggan thought it a splendid idea, and if you're worried about opting out for a few weeks, he can arrange that easily enough.'

What a neat, well-thought-out little plot, thought Samantha, too unhappy to speak for a moment. The invitation to choose household linen which Sappha could quite well have done on her own; the splendid lunch, the conversation which had included her throughout the meal, so that presumably she would feel one of their circle—they had made it impossible for her to refuse, and over and above this was the dreadful hurt of knowing that Giles loved Antonia. She said at length: 'May I think about it?'

'No,' said Giles at once. 'There's a good deal of arranging and so forth to be done and we want to know now, and if you're on the point of asking me what business it is of mine, I'll tell you at once that it's not, but Sappha is far too sweet to explain, and Rolf won't because she wouldn't like him to, so I will. These two are on their way to Scotland to stay for a few days with some old friends; if you keep them hanging around for an answer they'll not get there, and I happen to know that they want to go rather particularly.'

'I don't see why...' began Samantha, but was not allowed to finish.

'They have to see your Matron—a formality, I agree, but Doctor Duggan can't get on with the rest of the business until they do. They hoped that you would say yes today, so that they can visit her and be on their way.' He added carelessly, 'Once that's done, I can fix things with Duggan.'

All beautifully planned. It would be delightful to go to Holland, even though she wouldn't see much of Giles; when he came it would be to visit Antonia. Oh, she would meet him, of course, and he would give her a careless, smiling greeting, well aware that in some secret way of his own he had changed her initial dislike of him to one of liking. Loving was the word, but that was secret—and now, content with his easy conquest, he would make use of her. She sighed and said in a level voice: 'Thank you for making it all so clear. I'll make up my mind now and say yes.'

She was glad she had said that when she saw the happiness in Sappha's face, and the Baron, whose face was not easily to be read, looked pleased too. She wondered briefly why they wanted to go to Scotland so much and then addressed herself to Giles, her voice still nicely under control.

'You will let me know when you want me to go? I should like to go down to Langton Herring…about how long will I be away?'

The two men exchanged glances. 'A week—ten days,' suggested Rolf. 'We shall be going back before then—the practice, you know. Would you mind travelling alone with Antonia?'

'Not a bit.'

He nodded. 'Then we can leave it to Giles to sort things out and let you know dates and so on just as soon as he can.' He smiled again and Sappha said: 'Rolf, dear…'

'I almost forgot—your salary. Will you allow me to arrange that for you? I believe that you will have to come off the hospital payroll while you are with Antonia, so that you will receive your salary from me—and expenses, of course.'

Samantha thanked him a little shyly and said warm-heartedly to Sappha: 'I shall look forward to meeting you again and seeing your little son.'

'He's gorgeous,' said his doting mother. 'Do you know, the other day...' The two girls became immersed in the enthralling subject of babies and Sappha's baby in particular, while her husband sat back, looking pleased with himself, and Giles stared up at the ceiling, his placid expression giving away nothing of his thoughts. It was he who presently suggested that if they were to go back to Clement's they might be able to see the Matron without any further delay; his friends could then pay a quick visit to Antonia and be on their way. This idea was taken up immediately; Matron, tackled by both doctors, was quickly made to see the necessity for Antonia to have a suitable escort if she returned home, and the advantage of her nurse remaining for a short time until she was more herself. It could, she assured her visitors, be arranged—indeed, she was prepared to telephone Doctor Duggan at that very moment.

Sappha and Samantha, strolling up and down the hospital forecourt, were getting to know each other. 'You must be wondering why Rolf and I are so keen to go to Scotland,' said Sappha. 'We met there—in the Western Highlands, at a little place called Dialach, we got married there too. My mother-in-law's great friend is married to the minister there— you'd love the MacFees.' She gave Samantha a half laughing glance. 'I daresay you think we're wildly sentimental.'

'No, I don't, I think it sounds marvellous. I've never been to Scotland.'

Sappha tucked her arm into Samantha's. 'Then you must go some time. Things seem different there, it's like another world—I can't explain, but you'd know if you went.' She looked round. 'Here are the men, looking pleased with themselves.'

'All settled,' Rolf told them. 'About ten days' time, Samantha, if you can manage that and Tonia keeps her temp down. Matron has promised fair play about days off before you go. I'm leaving Giles to settle the details before he goes again. Is that OK?'

'Yes, thank you. I hope you both have a lovely holiday.' She shook hands. 'You're going up to see Tonia, aren't you?' She turned to Giles and offered him a hand too. 'Goodbye, Giles, you'll let me know what you've arranged later, I expect.'

She gave him a politely social smile which changed to a slightly frustrated look because he hadn't let her hand go again. 'Tea?' he asked, 'or dinner this evening?'

'I'm sorry, I'm not free this evening and I must get back to the flat—things to do...'

The other two had strolled away towards the hospital, so there was no one to hear when Giles said at his driest: 'The brush-off again, and I can't think why; I thought we were rather enjoying each other's company.' He sounded bland and a little amused and she felt her temper rising.

'I do have a life of my own,' she told him, 'and there was no need to go to all the trouble of chatting me up and giving me lunch and visiting your house, just to get me into the right mood to say I'd go back with Tonia.' She paused for breath and heard his silky: 'Well, well, what an outburst!' He took her by the arm, willy-nilly, and marched her to the hospital gates, where he hailed a taxi, put her in it, gave the driver her address and some money and then put his handsome head through the window, so that his face was only inches from hers.

'Enchanting Samantha,' he said in her outraged ear. 'Not beautiful, not even, I fear, pretty, but wholly enchanting.'

She was still framing a searing retort to this piece of impertinence when he withdrew his head and the taxi shot away.

Samantha was back in the flat when she remembered that the other three wouldn't be in that evening; Sue had wangled a half day so that she could go out with the new Casualty Officer, Joan had days off and Pam was on duty until nine o'clock. Samantha made a pot of tea and drank it from the mug in her hand as she mooned around the sitting room. The evening loomed, dreadfully dull, before her. She pictured Giles spending the greater part of it with Antonia; it must have been a great relief to him when she had refused his invitation to dinner, although she was sorry now that she hadn't agreed to have tea with him—it would have been an elegant meal, she felt sure, with tiny sandwiches, and mouth-watering cakes and tea in china cups. She re-filled her mug with the strong brew she had made against a threatening headache, and went to look for the biscuit tin.

There was that good old standby of washing her hair to fill the hour after tea, and then, because the bath water was hot, it seemed tempting providence not to use it. By half past seven she was dressing-gowned, with her hair flowing down her back, very clean and shining, and in the kitchen inspecting the cupboard's contents for her supper.

'A book,' she told herself out loud, 'and a hot water bottle and no one to disturb me.' It sounded so horribly dreary that she switched on the radio, and when Mr Cockburn's voice, shouting through the door, made itself heard at last, she shouted back: 'Come in, do—I suppose you want the rent.'

'Well, no,' said Giles, 'what I really want is my dinner and company in which to eat it, and as I never take no for an answer, I thought I would come and see if you had changed your mind.'

He stood before her, studying her at leisure from head to toe and then back again, while a variety of feelings swelled her bosom. It was disconcerting when he said: 'I like your hair—clean and straight and long.'

She opened and shut her mouth several times; surprise had scattered her wits and lost her her tongue, and what sort of an answer could she give to that, for pity's sake?

'Close your mouth, dear girl,' he begged her, 'and go and put on some clothes and we'll go somewhere quiet.'

Samantha was a good-tempered girl, prepared to be friendly with anyone, gentle-hearted and calm within reason; she was also possessed of a stubborn streak which seldom came to the surface. But it did now.

'I don't want to go out to dinner,' she stated, not mincing matters. 'I don't want to go anywhere quiet…' She paused because the doctor had sidled his bulk into the kitchen and was contemplating the tin of beans and the slice of bread already laid on the grill. 'Beans on toast?' he asked with loathing. 'You're not going to eat that for supper?' He shuddered and turned his back on the despised food. 'There's a very good place…' he began.

'No,' said Samantha, 'I won't.' She added as a polite afterthought, 'Thank you.'

He folded himself into a chair. 'Well, in that case, I'll have to spend the evening here.' He sounded quite pathetic, but she hardened her galloping heart.

'Oh, no, you don't,' she said firmly. 'You're just being ridiculous—you must have any number of friends with whom you could dine, and surely you know by now that half the nurses in Clement's would come running if you crooked a finger.'

'But not you, dear Sam.'

'No, not me.' She uttered the lie in a rather loud voice, hoping to convince herself as well as him.

'Then it will have to be the beans.'

She wrapped her dressing gown more closely around her. It was a woolly, sensible garment which Mrs Humphries-Potter had given her one Christmas and it wouldn't wear out and it was so roomily cut that she looked like a child bundled into a garment of its mother's. 'No,' she said once more.

'Oh, have you something else in the house?' He sounded hopeful.

Samantha said 'No' again, regretting the monotony of her conversation.

He looked resigned. 'Beans, then, and I'll make the coffee.'

'I don't think you quite understand,' she told him clearly.

'Oh, yes, I do. You're nothing but a turn-coat—only the other day you told me that you didn't dislike me any more, and here you are being so inhospitable that I wonder you can look me in the face.'

'Well,' she breathed indignantly, 'of all the…sitting there and…just wasting time. You could be visiting Tonia.'

She hadn't meant to say that; it had popped out and it was too late to do anything about it. She arranged her unremarkable features into a wooden calm and looked at him.

'So I could, only I've been with her ever since I left you and when her supper was brought in no one invited me to stay and share it with her.'

'All you think about is food,' said Samantha crossly.

'I'm a large man.' He got up suddenly and caught her by the shoulders. 'Now, having had your say, go and dress, girl. I have to return to Holland in the morning and I have a great deal to tell you before I go.'

She tried not to notice his hands. 'You could have said that right away.'

'So much on my mind,' his voice was suave, 'and it's impossible to hold two thoughts together when I'm with Tonia.'

Samantha said quietly: 'Of course. I'll go and dress, I won't be long.'

He had said somewhere quiet, which wasn't much help, although he was wearing a beautifully cut suit of fine grey cloth; she played safe and put on a plain brown wool dress and covered it with her almost new winter coat with a gay scarf tucked into its neck. Hardly eye-catching, she considered, surveying herself in the small mirror, but passable.

They went to Inigo Jones in Garrick Street, and she was relieved to find that even if she couldn't match the elegance of the other women in the restaurant, at least she merged nicely into the almost ecclesiastical background, with its arches and stained glass and wood carvings.

They ate Blinis au Saumon and followed that delicacy with Entrecote Minute Odessa, and it was over this that Giles began to tell her about the trip she was to undertake with Antonia.

'It's fixed up with the hospital—Duggan saw to that—they wanted to know how long you would be in Dokkum and I said two or three weeks—it might be a little longer than that, but if it is, Rolf will get in touch with Duggan in good time. You had better fly over; I daresay Tonia will be as sick as a dog, but you can cope with that, can't you? I'll arrange things so that there's no hanging around at the airport—you had better have an ambulance to get you there and someone to be on hand to get you aboard. You will be met at Schiphol, of course, and Tonia will have to go to bed for a day or so when she gets home—she's a volatile creature, quick to run a temperature. Have you outdoor uniform?'

She nodded. Clement's still retained its old-fashioned cape and funny little bonnet because it had been argued that the nurses stood less chance of being mugged if they were recognisable as being such.

'Then wear it, Samantha. It attracts the male eye as easily as a pretty face—you'll get more help.' He looked at her blandly as he spoke, but although this unfortunate remark nettled her, she wouldn't allow it to annoy her.

'Very well,' she said sedately. 'How do I get the tickets?'

'They will be sent to you, together with sufficient money for expenses on the journey.' He picked up the menu. 'Now, what about a sweet? There's a thing made of sponge and nuts and fruit and so forth—Tonia loves it.'

She would have to get used to the irritation she felt each time he mentioned Antonia's name. She would have to get used to the ache in her heart too. She said meekly that in that case she would like to try it and when it came, ate it with suitable enthusiasm, although it tasted of nothing but dust and ashes, making cheerful conversation as she did so.

It was late when they left the restaurant and St Paul's was striking midnight as he stopped the car outside the flat. 'I'd ask you in for coffee,' said Samantha, 'only Pam and Joan will be in bed, and besides, Mr Cockburn doesn't really like visitors after eleven o'clock.'

The doctor took no notice at all of this remark but got out of the car and went round its ultra-elegant bonnet to open her door. Half way up the steps, his hand tucked under her elbow, he stopped to raise an arm in greeting to the house owner, still, at that late hour, at his window. 'Does he count you as you come in?' he asked with interest.

Samantha, nicely aglow from the excellent claret they had had with their dinner, chuckled. 'Don't be absurd, he's only keeping a fatherly eye on us. Anyway, he's interested in the comings and goings; nothing very exciting happens to him, you see.'

The doctor turned her round to face him and put out a large hand to cup her firm little chin.

'Well,' he said slowly, 'this is hardly exciting, but at least it may brighten his dreams tonight.'

He bent and kissed her, taking his time about it, and giving common sense and wisdom a metaphorical kick, Samantha kissed him back before wishing him a slightly flurried good night and dashing up the rest of the steps at a fine rate.

She arrived at the flat door out of breath for more reasons than one to find Pam and Joan, dressing-gowned and hair imposingly imprisoned in rollers, waiting for her.

'Where have you been?' they hissed in chorus, and then stood back to look at her. 'All starry-eyed too! It's that doctor again, isn't it? The one with the Rolls—old Cocky told us...'

Samantha perceived that if she wished to get to her bed that night she would first of all have to satisfy her friends' curiosity. 'I went out to lunch,' she explained, 'to help Doctor ter Ossel choose sheets and pillowcases and things— he's got a house, close to Harrods.'

She ignored her companions' elaborately raised eyebrows and winks and nods. 'Antonia van Duyren's brother and his wife were there too. Then I came back here and—and he came round and asked me to have dinner with him.'

'At Stan's place down the road?' asked Pam with a grin.

'Well, no.' Samantha saw no point in holding anything back, for they would only ask more questions. 'We went to somewhere called Inigo Jones.'

She was stopped by shrill whistles from both her friends, and Pam said:

'Not only devastatingly good-looking and owning a Rolls but he eats out at all the best places. I suppose his house was one of those Mayfair places described as bijou residences, costing half a million.'

Samantha said in surprise: 'However did you know? Though I don't suppose it cost anything like that. It's so small, only three bedrooms.'

'Oh, so she went all over the place, did she?' uttered Joan. 'He means business, does he, ducky?' She studied Samantha's face closely. 'You are all starry-eyed,' she reiterated. 'Has he proposed?'

'No,' said Samantha, and it hurt her to say so, 'and he isn't going to either. If you must know, he's in love with Antonia.'

The effects of the claret had worn off, and she knew now exactly how Cinderella had felt when it struck midnight. 'I think I'll go to bed,' she said, in a voice devoid of all expression. Suddenly, standing there, keeping her end up with Joan and Pam had become quite intolerable. No doubt they found it all rather amusing, but for her there was no amusement at all.

She slept so badly that she got up early, made tea for all of them, and directly after breakfast offered to go to the launderette with the weekly load of washing, although it wasn't her turn; the other two were on duty at eleven, Sue had left early to be on duty at seven-thirty. There was nothing particular to do with her day off, the chore would fill in the morning nicely. Samantha marched off, walking briskly into the cold bright day, and left her two friends shaking their heads over her. They liked Samantha; she was cheerful, mostly good-tempered and quite unenvious of their succession of boy-friends, she was always ready to lend a sympathetic ear to their transitory romances and never once drew attention to the fact that she, although popular with everyone at Clement's, had no romances of her own. And now, they told each other worriedly, she had gone and fallen for someone who didn't care a button for her; just chatted her up for the fun of it because he had some time on his hands. Anyone listening to the two of them after she had gone might have supposed the doctor to be a man of unscrupulous nature and more than worthy of their dislike.

It was unfortunate for him that he should choose to call only half an hour after Samantha had left, burdened with her plastic bag of sheets and towels, and still more unfortunate that Mr Cockburn, for once, hadn't seen her go.

The doctor rang the flat bell, was admitted and in answer to his question as to Samantha's whereabouts, was assured that she had left very early that morning.

Giles wasn't the sort of man to show his feelings. He merely asked, placidly, where she was. 'I have to go back to Holland within an hour or so,' he explained, 'and I was hoping to see her before I left England.'

'Well,' said Pam, slowly, 'I don't suppose she would mind us telling you—she's gone out of London to spend the day with Jack.'

'Jack?' repeated the doctor with only the faintest air of wanting to know.

'Her fiancé,' Pam was well away by now. 'He managed to get a day off, so she's gone to Epping with him—that's where he lives.' She looked at him innocently as she fibbed.

He preserved an admirable calm at the news. 'Indeed?' he drawled, 'then I must be on my way.' He smiled at them both and as Pam afterwards put it, she felt a little mean because he looked rather nice. 'All the same,' she pointed out fiercely, 'I won't have our Sam's heart broken by some tycoon type who doesn't care a fig for her. That'll give him something to think about!'

As it had done. The doctor travelled back to Holland looking like a thundercloud, his black brows drawn together in a forbidding line above his handsome nose, ensuring that as few persons as possible spoke to him on the journey and then in a slightly apprehensive manner.

Samantha was glad to go back on duty the next day; the others had left the flat by the time she had got back from the launderette, to find a brief message telling her that Doctor ter Ossel had called but had left no message. She thought about him, on and off, for the rest of the day, for her inclination was to do nothing else, but by bedtime, common sense had prevailed. He had gone now; there had been nothing to prevent him leaving a message or even writing one, but he had done neither. She had made herself some coffee in lieu of lunch and spent the afternoon turning out her wardrobe; even if she was to travel in uniform, she would need other clothes. She piled what she possessed on her bed and hated the lot. A new outfit would have been splendid for her morale; after some thought she had decided that she would get herself another dress—purely for her own satisfaction, she had told herself and not for anyone else's—the anyone else being Giles. Even if she could have afforded half a dozen new dresses, he was hardly likely to notice them. Naturally he would come to see Antonia in Dokkum, but he was hardly likely to waste much time upon herself. How silly could she get, anyway, she apostrophized herself, worrying about making herself attractive to a man who couldn't care less? Had he not told her to her face that she wasn't pretty? An observation which still rankled even though she acknowledged it to be true.

She had gained no comfort from her friends when they returned that evening either, for their manner implied that although the doctor had called, his enquiries had been of the most casual, and they were emphatic that he had neither written a message nor had he wished to do so. Naturally enough, they said nothing about the fictitious Jack. Samantha had dismissed the matter from her mind; it had taken her the rest of the evening to do so.

Antonia was glad to see her back on duty, and was full of her return home. 'It is so nice that you come with me, Sam,' she declared happily. 'Rolf is also so pleased, he says that you are a nice girl.'

Samantha turned this lukewarm compliment over in her head and decided that it did nothing to improve her low spirits; probably Giles thought she was nice too as well as plain—a nonentity who would be unlikely to cause even the slightest ripple in the well-ordered pool of their lives. She said out loud, a thought snappish: 'Oh, I'm flattered,' and felt mean afterwards because Antonia thought that she had meant it.

The week passed, followed by a second, during which Antonia made steady progress. Her temperature had settled for three days now, and Doctor Duggan, during one of his impressive visits, declared that she might just as well go home.

'Probably there will be no need for you to remain for more than a day or so, Staff Nurse,' he advised Samantha, 'but should our patient have a recurrence of the fever then I presume that you are prepared to remain until such time as her doctor thinks fit.'

Samantha answered this prosy speech with a murmured 'Yes, sir.'

It was Sister Perkins who snapped: 'She'll stay—it's arranged,' in a manner which implied that she herself had suggested the whole thing in the first place. But she was kind enough about Samantha's days off before the journey to Friesland; no difficulty was placed in the way of her going home for two days on the understanding that she should be ready to go with her patient on the third day.

'Here at ten o'clock,' said Sister Perkins. 'Ambulance leaves at ten-fifteen. Collect notes, tickets and money before you go.'

So Samantha had travelled down after duty on her last evening, arriving well after nine o'clock at Weymouth, where she found Mr Humphries-Potter waiting for her. 'Your grandfather's getting a bit old for night driving,' he explained, 'and it seemed ridiculous to get a taxi when I had only to get the car out of the garage.'

A kindly act for which she was grateful even though it meant answering her companion's searching questions for the entire length of the journey. Her grandparents asked questions too, more gently put, it was true, and it wasn't until they were at breakfast the following morning that her grandmother asked: 'And that nice doctor we met—will you see him, I wonder, Sam dear?'

Samantha buttered toast. 'Very likely, I should think.' She took a large bite and steadied her voice to casualness. 'You see, Granny, he's in love with my patient.'

There was silence, then: 'And your patient—Antonia, isn't it, such a pretty name—is she in love with him?'

'I rather imagine so. She's years younger than he is, but she's very adult and intelligent, too. She's extremely pretty, too.' She added, determined to be quite fair: 'She'll be even prettier when she's got her usual complexion back again.'

Her grandfather cleared his throat, passed his cup for more tea, and remarked: 'She sounds eminently suitable to be the doctor's wife.'

Samantha took another bite, although she had no appetite any more. 'Oh, yes—you see her brother is Doctor ter Ossel's life-long friend—it couldn't be better.'

'They're engaged?' It was her grand-mother's turn.

'I don't know. I don't think so, but in any case I don't see any reason for either of them to tell me. I'm the nurse, darling.'

'And so nice for you, dear Sam, going off like this—it will be like a holiday for you, won't it?' Her grandmother smiled across the table at her. 'I know you'll have to work, but you will get a chance to look around you, I daresay.'

It was a good opening; Samantha launched into the possibilities of sightseeing while she was in Friesland; a safe topic which lasted for the remainder of breakfast. No one mentioned Giles ter Ossel again.

She took care to report early at the hospital; a good thing as it turned out, for Antonia, far too excited, had worked herself into a state of nerves which had caused her to refuse break-fast, ring the bell constantly for quite unnec-essary attention, and generally make a great nuisance of herself. The sight of Samantha in her quaint little bonnet and voluminous cape caused her to burst into tears, which she hastened to explain were because she was so re-lieved to see her again.

Samantha cast off her cloak, rolled up her sleeves and proceeded to wash her patient's face. 'A little lipstick,' she suggested, 'and a spot of mascara—put them on while I fetch your breakfast.'

'I don't want…' began Antonia.

'Yes, you do. Tea and toast, very thin and hot and dry—just the thing.' Samantha spoke bracingly as she sped to the kitchen to get it. She had Antonia dressed, the tea and toast con-sumed and everything ready for the journey by the time Sister Perkins sailed down the corri-dor to tell her that the ambulance man was on the way up.

There was a short delay while Antonia ar-gued hotly against being pushed in a wheel-chair. 'It's the wheelchair or staying here,' Samantha told her quietly, 'and you're being a bit silly, Tonia. Everyone's trying to help you to get home, and all you've done so far is to make it difficult.'

Her patient gave her a startled glance. 'Oh, Sam—I am not nice, no? I will do anything you say, for I wish to go home above all things.'

Samantha nodded her neat bonneted head. 'That's right,' she encouraged as she rang for the lift. The journey had begun; she hoped it would be a good one.

CHAPTER SIX

HER HOPE WAS only partly fulfilled. True, the journey from Clement's to the airport was a smooth one and there was no hitch in the transition of themselves and their luggage from that vehicle to the plane. With the minimum of formalities and a number of curious glances at the pretty girl with the slightly yellow face and her attendant nurse in her demure uniform, they were conveyed on board and settled in the rear of the cabin, where Baron van Duyren had had the forethought to book not only seats facing each other, but the seats alongside as well, so that Samantha was able to arrange the invalid comfortably at full length and spread a rug over her knees, while their impedimenta were disposed on the other vacant seat. But after such a promising start, things weren't so easy; the flight proved to be a bumpy one, and after a few minutes Antonia declared herself to feel sick, and sick she was, Samantha, her cape cast aside, did what she could to ease the situation.

They were over the Dutch coast by the time she had persuaded Antonia that a drink of hot, milkless tea would help her queasiness, and what with her efforts to get the drink down and the business of getting their seat-belts fastened, Samantha had no chance to so much as glance out of a porthole. Indeed, it surprised her to discover that they were actually taxiing down the runway at Schiphol, something which she saw with regret, for unlike poor Antonia, she had been looking forward to the flight, an event she had never experienced, and still in a way, hadn't. She tidied up her companion, coaxing her to smile again, and was glad to find that the same helpful and swift treatment was to be accorded them as in England. And waiting for them was Rolf van Duyren. Samantha, spotting him at a distance, tall and elegant, felt a wave of disappointment swallow her up; it was ridiculous of her to have hoped that Giles would be there, and even if he had been, he would have had no eyes for anyone but Antonia.

She waited while her patient hugged her brother, greeted him in her turn, and started on the business of getting Antonia comfortable in her brother's car. The journey had been short and it was still only early afternoon, but Antonia was flagging visibly. Samantha explained about the sickness as they sped along the motorway, leaving the airport behind, by-passing den Haag, and making for Leiden.

'Did she keep anything down?' her brother wanted to know.

'Some tea—she ate very little breakfast.' She saw him looking at her in the driver's mirror and when he smiled briefly, smiled back. She had Antonia's head on her shoulder, her arm around her. Her eyes were closed, but when Samantha said: 'Possibly she's asleep now,' she opened them and said: 'No, I'm not. I'm so thirsty, Rolf, please could we stop for a drink?'

They were almost in Leiden. Samantha found time to look around her and wished very much that she could have had more leisure— perhaps on her way back...

'We'll stop in Haarlem,' the Baron promised. 'Giles will give us tea—but only for a short time, mind, Tonia, then home and bed.'

Antonia opened her eyes again to stare up at Samantha's outwardly calm face. 'Just what I would wish,' she explained, and smiled quite gaily.

They were on the motorway once more, devouring the miles between Leiden and Haarlem and going very fast, but not fast enough for Samantha; she was going to see Giles again, after all; never mind if he hardly spoke to her—just to see him would be something. She remembered now, very clearly, how when she had been a little girl she had wanted a particular doll in a shop window—a large, extravagantly dressed doll with a quantity of fair hair and very expensive. Her mother had told her that it was quite impossible for her to have it; that it was far too costly, but that there were other dolls. Samantha recalled the fit of tantrums she had had when she discovered she wasn't going to get her own way, tantrums which had dissolved into sobs before long, until, quite tired out, her mother had sat her on her knee until she had become amenable to gentle argument. 'You see, Samantha,' her mother had told her, 'you can't always have what you want, so instead of crying for it you must learn to smile and make do with something almost as good, or do without.'

Samantha stared out of the car's windows at the approaching suburbs of Haarlem. There wasn't anyone almost as good as Giles, and there never would be; she would have to do without and smile about it. The city's suburbs were pleasant, with small villas set amongst neat, still wintry gardens, but the city itself was old, its great church of St Bavo dominating the picturesque old houses around it. The Rolls purred across the Grote Markt, turned off to the left of it over a canal, dawdled down a busy thoroughfare lined with tall, narrow houses and turned again into a narrow cobbled street with a canal down its centre. Half way down it the Baron manoeuvred the car under an arched gateway into a small, narrow courtyard, and stopped before a ponderous door, studded with nails. 'Stay there,' he commanded the girls, and got out to thump its great knocker, and then, not waiting for an answer, opened the door and disappeared inside. He reappeared almost immediately with Giles, who poked his head through the open door of the car with a cheerful hullo, and without further ado scooped Antonia up and carried her indoors. Samantha following more slowly with the Baron, saw him disappear through a door at the end of the short, dark passage they had entered.

'This is the side entrance,' explained her companion, as he opened the door for her to go through. 'The front door overlooks the canal, but we can't leave the car there; the street's too narrow.'

He was leading the way across the hall now, a wainscoted apartment with narrow leaded windows, an elaborate ceiling and a quantity of portraits hung upon its walls; there were a couple of high-backed armchairs too, a console table and a very large wall clock, and it was nicely dim and cosily warm. Samantha guessed central heating, although she could see nothing so modern. The room they followed Giles into was small and dark panelled like the hall, but here there was a bright fire burning, comfortable chairs scattered around on a deep, soft carpet, a magnificent display cabinet along one wall and leaded windows again, but this time far more of them, curtained in the same faded pinks and blues and greens of the carpet. Giles had dumped Antonia without ceremony on to a large sofa facing the fire, and turned to address Rolf as they crossed the room to join him.

'Tea, I take it? Isn't that the reason for this visit?' He looked laughingly at Antonia. 'Or was it for love of me?'

'Both,' she answered, her tiredness quite disappeared. 'I was very sick coming over, wasn't I, Sam?'

Both men looked at Samantha, still very neat although perhaps a trifle pale. 'And how is Samantha?' Giles wanted to know, and he was sure she detected mockery in his voice. Certainly his smile, as he allowed his slow gaze to travel slowly over her cloaked person and settle finally upon her little bonnet, was mocking. He said softly: 'Enchanting,' and the Baron said at once and smoothly: 'Yes, isn't

it? Such a pity that all hospitals haven't kept
their old uniforms. I love that bonnet; Sappha
will envy it with all her heart, I'm sure.'

Doctor ter Ossel's grey gaze went from
Samantha's bonnet to her face; his stare was
so intense that she felt the pink creeping into
her cheeks. She would have liked to have
looked away, but his eyes compelled her not
to, and all at once his smile wasn't mocking
at all. The spell, if spell it were, was broken
by the opening of the door and he said at once:
'Here is tea, and someone you know,
Samantha.'

It was Juffrouw Boot, dressed severely in
black, her ugly, nice face wreathed in smiles.
She put the tray on the Pembroke table by the
sofa, spoke to the company in general and then
addressed herself to Samantha.

'Nice,' she began, and frowned in thought.
'Good, also, Nurse Fielding.' And having exhausted her English she began again, in Dutch.

The doctor obligingly translated. 'Klara says
that she is so happy to see you again,' he told
Samantha. 'Her hands are better, she does almost everything with them.' He added with a

faint smile: 'She finds you very pretty in your cape and bonnet.'

'You're very kind,' Samantha told Juffrouw Boot uselessly. 'It's very nice to see you again.' They shook hands and smiled and nodded at each other and when the housekeeper had gone, she took off her cloak and went to pour the tea at her host's request.

They stayed only a very short time and Giles had little to say to her; a casual remark about their flight, a word or two about Clement's. She replied suitably and a little coldly because she was so afraid that he might discover her feelings, drank her tea and when her patient was ready, walked beside her as she went slowly across the lovely room with Giles' arm around her. But in the hall her brother whisked her off her feet and carried her out to the car, leaving Samantha and Giles behind. The doctor stopped, and she, out of politeness, stopped too.

'You must visit me again,' he remarked pleasantly. 'Klara will want to see you.'

'That would be nice, but I don't expect to be in Holland for more than a week or so.'

'In that case we must arrange something without delay.'

She clasped her hands tidily in front of her. 'Well, yes—perhaps.' And then, because he was still standing there, saying nothing more: 'I expect you will be coming to Dokkum to see Antonia?'

'Antonia?' He sounded faintly surprised. 'Oh, undoubtedly.' He had moved nearer to her. 'I imagine it will be another week at least before she feels quite herself again.' He put out a hand and tilted her chin and looked into her face. 'I think that perhaps you should make up your mind to remain a little longer, although of course you want to get back as quickly as possible. Do you not say ''Absence makes the heart grow fonder?'''

Samantha thought confusedly that he was talking about Clement's, or possibly her home in Dorset. 'Yes, oh, yes,' she agreed with rather more fervour than she felt.

He didn't answer her, only bent his head to kiss her mouth and then smile wickedly at her. 'It's that fetching bonnet,' he told her blandly.

She set her mouth firmly because it was shaking a little, and set off towards the door, where, under the dark eye of the Baron and Antonia's blue gaze, she wished Giles good-bye in an austere little voice, a gesture entirely spoiled by the fact that he didn't release her hand, but held it firmly while he discussed the probable visit he would make to Dokkum. Only when he had finished did he let go of her hand, open the car door and usher her in. She didn't look at him as they drove away but she could still feel his kiss.

Antonia was tired again; Samantha made her comfortable against her shoulder and presently she went to sleep, leaving Samantha to look out upon the darkening landscape, answer the Baron's occasional remarks, and discipline her thoughts, which were a horrid muddle of excitement, happiness and downright misery.

There was a warm welcome for them in Dokkum; the elderly Baroness van Duyren lived in a pleasant house on the edge of the little town and only a short distance from her son, who turned the car into the strip of a road leading to the canal which encircled Dokkum and stopped outside a door set in a high brick wall. 'The back way,' he informed Samantha, 'but much nearer the house.'

As indeed it proved to be, for the door opened on to a short covered passage which led directly into a roomy, old-fashioned kitchen. Rolf van Duyren strode through it with his sister, only half awake, in his arms, and Samantha half trotted behind, trying to keep up. A series of short passages opened out into what was presumably the front hall and the Baron, crossing it without shortening his stride, pushed open one of the doors in it and entered a rather sombre apartment, splendidly furnished and lighted by a number of wall sconces. Its two occupants rose to their feet as he went in—Sappha and an elderly lady, small and silver-haired and still pretty: Antonia's mother.

There was an outbreak of talk while Antonia was settled in a chair and the Baron greeted his wife and mother and introduced the latter lady to Samantha, but he allowed little time for the ladies to get to know each other, for he declared in a no-nonsense voice: 'Bed, Tonia,' and bore her off upstairs to a room on the first floor, a charming room which appeared to contain every comfort which a girl could wish for.

'You'll see to her?' he asked Samantha. 'Your room is next door and there's a bathroom on the other side of the landing. Sappha will show you round presently—you must excuse my mother from doing that, she isn't very strong.'

Left with her patient, Samantha took off her bonnet and cloak, rolled up her sleeves and began the task of helping Antonia to undress, bathed and into bed with as much speed as possible. Half an hour later the Dutch girl was sitting up against her pillows, looking tired and a little flushed, but not, Samantha thought, much the worse for her journey. True, her temperature was up a little, as was her pulse; a couple of days in bed would put that right, though. Samantha switched on the bedside light, fetched some magazines from the pile on the drum table by the window, and went off to find her own room.

It was a pleasant place, nicely warmed against the last of winter's cold; its pink curtains pulled to shut out the dark, the electric fire already glowing, the bed turned down and a bright-faced girl unpacking her case. Samantha, who had never had anyone to unpack for her before, was rather taken aback, but the girl smiled and nodded and went on putting undies and stockings away in the long row of drawers behind the cupboard doors, so Samantha hung up her cape and tidied herself at the dainty dressing table, and went back to Antonia. 'Supper?' she suggested. 'Something easy to eat, for you're tired, aren't you?'

She was on her way to the door when it was opened by Sappha. She smiled at them both, enquired how the invalid did and begged Samantha to accompany her downstairs. 'Rolf's on his way up,' she explained, 'just to say good night to Tonia, then we're going home. My mother-in-law hopes you'll have dinner with her after you've seen to Tonia.'

She went over to the bed and kissed her sister-in-law with affection, wished her a restful night, and joined Samantha again.

Downstairs, they made their way to the kitchen, where there was a tray ready for the invalid, and Sappha, seeing Samantha's surprised look, said pleasantly: 'You'll find you'll not have much to do—Rolf and his mother have a small posse of faithful servants who have been with them for ever—you will only have to lift your finger.' She glanced sideways at Samantha. 'Giles is in the same happy position—did you like his house?'

'Well, I didn't see a great deal of it—it looked quite delightfully old.'

'It is. It rambles all over the place, but he's happy in it; it's been in his family for a very long time and he hates to be away from it. That house in London, that was charming too, wasn't it? but I doubt if he uses it much. When he marries, of course, things will be different.'

Samantha longed to ask why and decided against it; it would do her no good to know. She said instead: 'It was a dear little house. Do you live close by?' And nothing more was said about Giles.

A week went by and Samantha hardly noticed its passing. There was very little nursing to do for Antonia, but nonetheless she needed companionship and constant encouragement, for she had reached the doldrums of convalescence, when no apparent progress was being made. After the first two days in bed she was up and about, showing Samantha around the house, talking endlessly to her mother and playing with Leo the Peke. It was Samantha who suggested to the family doctor when he called that perhaps she might take her patient for a drive each day, for although Rolf van Duyren had been over to fetch them to his own home, he was a busy man, and Sappha although she called most days, had a busy life of her own. She had brought baby Rolf to tea one day—a large, dark baby with miniature satyr's eyebrows, like his father. He had the same calm air, too, sitting happily on any lap which might be offered.

The visit to Sappha's home had been pleasant too, for Samantha, having seen Antonia nicely settled by the sitting room fire in the Baron's house, had accompanied Sappha on a tour of inspection round the old house, enjoying an interesting chat about clothes and babies, interspersed with snippets of nursing gossip while they examined the more interesting treasures around them before rejoining Antonia for tea round the fire.

Of Giles there had been no word; it wasn't until a week had gone by that Antonia casually mentioned that she had had a telephone call from Haarlem each day. 'While you were out for your afternoon walk,' she explained to Samantha.

'How nice,' remarked Samantha for lack of anything better to say, and added, fishing for news: 'Doctor ter Ossel will see a great difference in you when he comes.'

'Giles? Oh, he's always so busy—he's got such a large practice, you know, and a great deal of hospital work besides, but I daresay he'll contrive to come.' She sounded very sure of this, and Samantha felt a pang of pure envy and suppressed it at once. There was no point in making the situation worse for herself than it was already; if she pretended hard enough that she didn't care twopence for Giles, it might become true. Besides, any day now, she expected to be told that she was no longer required. She finished writing up Antonia's chart

which she kept meticulously for Doctor de
Winter when he called, changed into the despised tweed and a sweater, threw on her raincoat and a headscarf without much regard to
her appearance, and went out into the rain.
There was nothing like a good brisk walk to
clear the mind.

But her mind was no clearer when Giles arrived the following morning, just as Antonia,
wearing a new suede outfit, arrived downstairs.
Samantha, who had stayed behind to make the
bed, put away the medicines in a safe place
and tidily bestow the numerous bottles and jars
Antonia had used during the course of her toi-
lette, went downstairs herself a little later, to
find him in the sitting room, sharing a pot of
coffee with Antonia. He got to his feet as she
went in and smiled wryly as she checked in
the doorway, saying: 'Oh, good morning,' and
then as inspiration struck her: 'I'm so glad
you're here to entertain Tonia, for I did want
to go out this morning.'

'Then we mustn't keep you.' His voice was
bland, as was the expression on his face; she
suddenly wished very much that she could run

across the room to him and fling herself into his arms and tell him that what she really wanted to do was to stay with him, preferably for ever.

She slipped out of the room and upstairs to the Baroness with a fictitious story of wishing to explore the countryside to the north of the town, and as it was a dry day and Antonia had Doctor ter Ossel to bear her company, would it not be an excellent opportunity to go?

The Baroness, writing letters at her elegant little davenport under the window, agreed immediately, nodding her silver-fair head in agreement while her sharp eyes studied Samantha's face. 'I expect Giles will take Tonia down to Haarlem,' she mentioned, 'so don't hurry back—I'll ask the kitchen to give you whatever you would like when you get in.'

Samantha tore into her clothes, knotted her headscarf with a ferocious tug and got into her boots. She could not, she told herself, get out of the house fast enough, away from Giles, who had seemed quite anxious to be rid of her. She sniffed to prevent tears, and hurried out of the house.

It was cold with an overcast sky and the wind blowing as it always blew; a thoroughly miserable day. She walked briskly along the Ooster Singel and crossed the little bridge over the encircling canal, and took the road running straight ahead of her. She had little idea of where it led, and she really didn't care; the signpost had said Oostrum, and the road was little more than a lane running between the flat empty fields.

When she reached Oostrum she found it to be a very small village indeed, and although it boasted a café and she longed for coffee, she didn't like to go inside—coffee, she had already discovered, sounded the same in both languages, but supposing someone started talking? The Dutch language meant nothing to her as yet, save for a few words she had picked up when she had gone to the post office in Dokkum. She left the village behind with regret and when she came to the fork in the road just beyond it, decided to take the right hand, which led to the village of Ee, a name which she found so intriguing that it seemed well worth a visit. But Ee was disappointing, being but a large church and a handful of cottages; it was on a good road, though, and she took the one pointing towards Dokkum, although the signpost omitted to mention how far she had to go, but it was barely midday and she was in no hurry; she certainly didn't want to get back before Giles had left with Antonia.

The road was narrow and lonely, with wide views in all directions. She began to walk along it, so deep in thought that she failed to notice the gathering gloom of the sky. The first raindrops didn't bother her overmuch, although when she stopped and looked behind her, the threatening clouds galloping in her direction took her by surprise. There was no house nearby, indeed, a scattering of farms, some way off, were all the signs of habitation there were to be seen. Samantha walked a little faster—a tree, or even a high hedge, would give some shelter, only there was neither, only flat fields and little canals and an occasional gate. Before long she was very wet indeed and bad-tempered with it; the rain was pelting down now; it ran coldly down the back of her neck, lacquered her tights to her legs and trickled on to fill her boots with wetness. She wiped her eyes with the back of a hand and examined the signpost by the side of the road—it pointed to Oostwoud, but she wasn't sure any more if that had been the name of the village she had passed through earlier. The road ahead had no signpost at all; she hesitated for a moment and turned into a side road; it must surely be the same village; if the rain hadn't been falling like a heavy curtain, she would be able to see Dokkum ahead of her.

The village, when she reached it ten minutes later, wasn't the one she had expected it to be, though, and although she might have sought shelter in its one silent street, there seemed little point, for she was already soaked to the skin. There was no change in the wide bowl of sky around her, it was as black and threatening as ever, so she plodded on, meeting no one, since no one with any sense would be out in such weather. She had walked another mile when she came upon an old-fashioned milestone which informed her in carved letters that she was on her way to Dantumawoude, a name she found difficult to pronounce, let alone place in her scanty knowledge of the district. A little reckless by now, because she was quite lost, she took the next turning she came to, apparently leading to nowhere, but feeling as she did, it seemed to her that anywhere would be better than the place with the unpronounceable name. But after half a mile of further walking, doubts began to creep in, for the horizon, what Samantha could see of it, appeared free of all habitation; it lost itself in the flat, rainswept distance which she found increasingly depressing, a depression made worse by the thought that by now Giles would be back in his home, and Antonia with him.

Only he wasn't. The Merlin swooped silently from behind and caught her quite unawares. Samantha stood, her scarf plastered to her head, her face dripping, staring at him openmouthed as he pulled up beside her and pressed an impatient finger on the knob which would wind down the car's window. When it was fully open, he said with icy pleasantness across the space between them: 'What the hell are you doing?'

She perceived that he was in a rage, a sight which stoked her own inflamed feelings. 'I came out for a walk,' she told him haughtily, and when he received this with a derisive snort, added by way of explanation: 'I wanted to explore.'

His brows were a straight, furious line above a nose and mouth cut from stone. 'Get in,' he said, his voice still pleasant, and if possible, icier. 'I'll drive you back.'

She longed above all things to get out of the rain—he had the door open, but she hung back, the warmth of her emotions welded into a fine stubbornness.

'I'm too wet, I shall spoil your car—besides, you're in a frightful temper.' She glowered at him and tried to catch the raindrops at the corners of her mouth with the tip of her tongue. 'I don't care to go with you.'

The straight mouth twitched, the grey eyes were alight with laughter.

'It doesn't matter about you being wet and I shan't bite.' He opened the door a little further. 'Get in, or are you afraid to do so?'

Her chin went up. 'Certainly not,' she told him indignantly, and got in. She was barely seated before he shot off at a fine pace.

There seemed little point in conversation; Samantha sat dripping little pools on to the expensive leather of her seat. Presently she shivered.

'You've probably caught your death of cold,' Giles remarked without turning to look at her. 'It would serve you right.'

It was ridiculous to be so upset; tears trickled down her cheeks, mixed in with the rivulets of rain still meandering down her face from her hair.

'Why are you crying?' His voice was sharp.

She swallowed the tears and found her voice. 'I'm not crying—my face is wet with rain.' Just to let him see how utterly normal she was feeling, she went on: 'I thought you would be in Haarlem—the Baroness said…'

'I've just come back from there.' He sounded impatient. 'Baroness van Duyren was worried because you hadn't come back. It's a good thing for you that the country is open enough for anyone to see you a mile away.'

She agreed with him, her voice a little forlorn, and thanked him meekly for coming to look for her, and as he made no reply to this, she sat silent again as he swept the car over the bridge and into Dokkum once more. In the house, he bade her go upstairs and take off her things and have a hot bath, and without waiting to see if she intended to obey his somewhat arbitrary orders, turned his back on her and went into the sitting room.

Samantha went downstairs half an hour later, in her uniform once more, very neat and composed, a suitable apology for the inconvenience she had caused him ready on her tongue. Only he had gone; the Baroness, after enquiring kindly after her, volunteered the information that he had business with Rolf and as soon as it was concluded, would go back to Haarlem. 'To fetch Tonia,' she concluded. 'Such a lot of travelling to and fro, poor boy, but the dear child had set her heart on going and he promised her…'

Promised her what? wondered Samantha as she set up the card table in answer to an invitation to play bezique with her companion, and went on wondering throughout the game, so that her play was indifferent to say the least.

'We'll have tea, shall we?' murmured the Baroness.

'I'm afraid you will have to put up with my company for dinner this evening, for Tonia won't be back until late. If I weren't so sure that Giles would take good care of her, I would not have allowed her to go.'

Samantha accepted a cup of tea and took a comforting sip, only it held no comfort. The day, she decided, nibbling a paper-thin biscuit with no appetite, had been horrible.

CHAPTER SEVEN

ANTONIA DIDN'T ARRIVE home until almost midnight; she came in with Giles, bubbling over with good spirits. It seemed to Samantha, who had waited up for her, that her convalescence was quite over, she looked radiant and very attractive. All the same, she yawned prettily as they entered the sitting room, declaring that she was exhausted.

'But you shouldn't have waited up for me, dear Sam,' she expostulated. 'I feel marvellous.' She turned to Giles, who had said nothing. 'Darling Giles,' she flung her arms around him and kissed him, 'how would I manage without you—and now everything is perfect.'

He smiled down at her. 'I'm glad of that, Tonia. And now off to bed with you, or Samantha will become a stern martinet.'

Antonia didn't know what a martinet was, and when Giles told her, she found it very funny indeed that her dear Sam should be anything so severe. Samantha laughed too, because she could see that she was expected to, although she had found nothing amusing in his remark; she was further incensed by him saying carelessly: 'She can be, you know—the first time we met at Clement's, she terrified me.'

Antonia gave a gurgle of laughter. 'Giles, you talk nonsense, I think, and perhaps you annoy my Sam, and that you must not do.'

The doctor had gone to sit on the arm of one of the easy-chairs. He agreed with a grave face that he must certainly do no such thing, but Samantha, casting him a lightning glance, knew that he was laughing silently and fumed, although her voice was pleasantly composed.

'It's lovely to see you so happy, Tonia. Doctor de Winter is going to be pleased with you when he comes tomorrow.'

Antonia clapped a beautifully kept hand over her mouth. 'I had forgotten—but he will only look at me this time, will he not? and say that I am well—I am well, you know.'

Samantha looked at Giles before she replied: 'I imagine so, but I'm not the one to decide that.'

'Well, I am, I know it. Giles, you are to say so.'

'I'm not your doctor, my dear. Let us first hear what de Winter has to say, although I shall be surprised if he doesn't pronounce you quite cured.'

Antonia had subsided into a chair. 'This is nice—I can hardly wait. Only there is a sad thing—if I am well, my dear Sam will go away.'

'Ah, yes,' said Giles, smoothly interrupting her, 'which makes it imperative that we make the arrangement for you to visit me, Samantha.' He got up and strolled across the room. 'Let us see, today is Thursday. I am free on Sunday, so I will fetch you at about nine o'clock. Will that suit you?'

She could find no words with which to squash this high-handed arrangement even while her heart jumped with delight at the thought of it. She managed: 'Well, but...'

He gave her no chance to finish, which was a good thing, for her thoughts were incoherent. 'I imagine you are hardly likely to leave for England before then,' his voice was pleasantly casual, 'and you must certainly not return without having seen a little of Holland.'

She was unable to deny this; visitors to strange countries were expected to jump at any chance offered to show them the local sights of interest, but it didn't matter in the least that she made no reply, for Antonia was speaking.

'Of course you will go, Sam. Giles shall fetch you as he says he will, and he will guide you round and perhaps show you his house too, which is beautiful.' She got up. 'So that is all arranged.'

She walked across to where Giles was standing and put her face up to be kissed, wished him goodnight and started for the door. 'I shall take a bath, Sam,' she declared as she went, 'and then you will make me comfortable in my bed as you always do and stand over me while I swallow my pills, will you not?'

She beamed at them both and went out of the room and Samantha made to go after her, to be frustrated by the doctor, who, by the simple expedient of putting his large frame between her and the door, effectively prevented her.

'I think I had better go upstairs and just make sure that Tonia…' she began, wishing most fervently that she need do no such thing.

He ignored this poor attempt at escape on her part. 'Is there anywhere you would particularly like to go to on Sunday?' he asked.

'Well—no, may I leave it to you? You—you're sure you can spare the time? I mean, I could go off on my own quite easily.'

It was a mistake to have said that, for he said dryly: 'Yes, but you don't seem very good at getting yourself back again, do you?' He was smiling now, without mockery. 'Of course I can spare the time; I'm free on Sunday, excepting for an odd call or so, and I can fit those in as we go. And we must save some time for Klara, who wants to talk to you.' He added slowly: 'Your stay has been a short one.'

'Yes, I didn't expect it to last very long, though. It's been like a holiday.'

His dark brows shot up. 'Indeed? Hardly my idea of leisure—you have not had much time to yourself, have you?'

'As much as I wanted,' she answered sharply.

To which he replied mildly, 'Well, there's no need to get so uppity about it.'

'I'm not uppity!' Her voice was regrettably shrill, and he grinned.

'I'll go, but I shall be back on Sunday, and mind you're in a good mood, Sam.' He took her arm and walked her across the hall to the door. 'Will you lock up after me?' He let her go and shrugged himself into his coat and picked up his gloves as she put a hand on the old-fashioned brass door handle. He removed it gently. 'Oh, but first we say good night,' he murmured, and kissed her. The next moment he had opened the door and gone.

She lay awake a long while that night, thinking about him. The kiss, of course, had been out of gratitude; Antonia was well again, now they could make plans for their wedding; anyone or anything who had had a hand in hastening that event would be entitled to a show of gratitude—besides, she was aware that men kissed girls, even plain ones if there were no pretty ones around, if they happened to be feeling like it.

If she hadn't loved him so much, it wouldn't have mattered at all. She reminded herself of this and fell to thinking of other things. She would have to write to Clement's and tell them that she would be returning very shortly, which led, naturally enough, to speculation as to which ward she would be sent to—not PP, she hoped—probably on night duty again as she was expected to apply for the Night Sister's post in a few weeks' time. She attempted to cheer herself up with the thought of the extra money she would earn and the possibility of advancement to Senior Night Sister, even, in the course of years, Night Superintendent. She tossed about in her comfortable bed, sickened at the very idea. Perhaps she should get another job instead of taking the new post—somewhere and something quite different where she would meet fresh faces and learn new work, but she didn't like that idea either. She closed her eyes resolutely, and immediately Giles was there, under their lids. With a sigh she sat up, switched on her bedside light and opened a book, reading the same page over and over again without seeing a word of it and at last dropping off to sleep, the book still open in her hands.

In the morning Doctor de Winter pronounced Antonia cured. 'A little care,' he advised, 'no overtaxing of your strength and not too many late nights.' He twinkled nicely at his pretty patient. 'I shall see Rolf before I go and he will make sure that you come to no harm.'

Antonia tossed her head. 'I am now grown-up,' she spoke in her elegant stilted English, 'and he does not need to worry about me.'

'Well, not for much longer,' conceded the doctor. 'I daresay he will be glad to see you married.' He chuckled at his little joke, made some kindly remark to Samantha, and presently, after he had visited the Baroness, took his leave. Over coffee, Antonia was jubilant. 'Now I am well, just as Giles said. Now I need no longer take care, dear Sam, nor shall I rest after lunch—if only you were staying longer we could have gone shopping together—den Haag, I think, there are some good shops there. But you will be gone.'

Samantha agreed that this was so. Directly Doctor de Winter had gone she had gone to the Baroness and asked when she should leave, fired with the idea that she should make an effort to avoid meeting Giles again, much though she wanted to; but that kindly lady would have nothing of it and dissuaded her from packing her bags and catching the next train.

'I'm sure that you wish to get back to your hospital,' she said, with erroneous kindness, 'but please, Samantha, you will stay just a few more days. Until—let us say Tuesday? Then you will have your day out with Giles and a day to pack your things and say goodbye to us all. It is already Friday and Sappha telephoned just now to ask us all to go to dinner on Saturday, and then perhaps you would drive Antonia and me to Leeuwarden tomorrow or Sunday—we will go in the Mini which you drive very well, far better than Tonia, who frightens me very much.' She smiled coaxingly. 'You will wish to buy presents.'

So it had been arranged; her last few days were already planned for her and she didn't care much; she would enjoy going to Sappha's house again, although she wasn't sure if the dress she had brought with her was quite good enough. And it would be fun to go to Leeuwarden. She didn't allow herself to think about Sunday, or after that, but agreed cheerfully to the Baroness's suggestions and entered into Antonia's plans for the afternoon with suitable enthusiasm before going off to write a letter to her grandmother.

Her dress, when she put it on on Saturday evening, seemed a poor thing. It was a silk jersey, the colour of claret and very plain, and because she had had it for two years, she found it dull. Yet it suited her; the colour lent her soft hair a gleam and it was an excellent fit. She turned and twisted before the pier glass in her bedroom and at length, dissatisfied, went downstairs, to feel even more so when Antonia appeared, clad in a sapphire blue velvet skirt, a crêpe blouse with huge sleeves and a brocade waistcoat. She looked quite beautiful, and Samantha told her so and meant it. They were joined shortly by Baroness van Duyren, wearing something black and crêpey and looking as pretty as her youngest daughter. She accepted their admiration gracefully and then astonished Samantha by remarking that although she might not be a pretty girl, any man would certainly take a second look at her.

A remark which sent Samantha's ego soaring, so that when the Baron arrived to drive them over, she actually believed him when he too remarked on her charming appearance. It was only when they reached his house, to be greeted by Sappha and introduced to a number of other guests, that Samantha admitted to herself that she had hoped—expected—that Giles would be there too. But despite her disappointment she enjoyed herself; her dinner partner, thoughtfully selected by Sappha, was young, unmarried and pleasant-mannered, even if his English was pedantic in the extreme. It was a pity, thought Samantha crossly, that her love for Giles should prevent her from appreciating him, especially as he gave every indication of liking her.

And in the drawing room later, she found herself in conversation with another young man, tall and rugged-faced and very fair. He had partnered Antonia at dinner and Samantha had noticed them talking together frequently during the evening; she had wondered why until he told her who he was. Doctor ter Ossel's houseman at the hospital, he introduced himself with some pride and in perfect English, and proceeded to eulogize his chief for some minutes. Giles, she was informed earnestly, was a brilliant physician, a clever man besides and a wonderful boss, although his wrath—a righteous wrath, it was explained to her, in case she got the wrong impression—was to be feared when meted out to those who deserved it.

'He plays rugger too, even though he is no longer young,' ended her companion, putting, as it were, a verbal crown on his venerable hero's head.

Samantha showed suitable surprise, and anxious to keep the conversation going about

Giles, remarked that she had expected to see him there that evening, since he was such a close friend of the van Duyrens. Her companion's reply took her very much by surprise.

'But that would have been impossible—he wishes to be free tomorrow, and in order to be so he has taken over Doctor van Toren's ''on call'' for the hospital this evening—there is always a consultant to be reached, you understand— thus Doctor van Toren will stand in for him tomorrow.'

Samantha digested this news with mixed feelings and she was on the point of asking a few searching questions, the answers to which she dearly wished to know, when Antonia joined them.

'You talk so earnestly,' she remarked gaily. 'Why is that?'

Samantha explained, adding: 'It must be disappointing for you, Tonia and I feel very guilty about it, for if Giles hadn't asked me to go out tomorrow he could have been here this evening.'

'Pooh! What is a little dinner party compared with a whole day of seeing sights?'

Antonia wanted to know. 'It is your only chance of seeing a little of Holland before you return. I think it is a splendid idea,' she added handsomely, 'and I told Giles so.'

'Well—' said Samantha, glad that Antonia didn't object but still not very happy about it, and not sure either that she would enjoy the outing in the circumstances, but she got no further, for Doctor de Winter joined them and engaged her in conversation about Clement's, and presently her dinner partner sought her out again.

The guests gone, Samantha found herself sitting round the fire in the drawing room, drinking a final cup of coffee while the dinner party was casually discussed by her host and hostess, the Baroness and Antonia.

'A very pleasant evening,' pronounced Rolf lazily. 'You have a happy knack of collecting together people who like each other, my love.'

He stretched his long legs to the blaze and the look he gave his wife was one of such devotion that Samantha, looking up and catching it, felt a pang of sorrow that Giles would never look at her like that. Perhaps her feelings showed on her face, for Sappha got up and went to sit beside her.

'You liked Henk, Samantha? He's rather a dear, I think, and such an interesting job—research chemistry. He liked you.'

Samantha said a little obscurely: 'Yes, I know—such a pity, he really was so very nice…'

Sappha gave her a thoughtful glance. 'But second best. I think you're like me, Samantha, you would rather have nothing if you can't have what you want.'

Samantha looked at her in horror. 'Oh—did I say that? I didn't mean—that is, yes, I suppose you're right.'

Sappha made no attempt to sort this out but went on briskly: 'You haven't had much chance to get around, have you? I never did either, though I had a passion for the museum, I was always in and out, the curator has become our good friend.' She smiled gently and Samantha, who had been told by the Baroness that Sappha had nursed her before she had married Rolf, wished she knew more of their story. She was on the point of putting a suitably casual question about this when the Baroness remarked that it was time that they went home and the little family party broke up.

'Come and say goodbye,' begged Sappha. 'I'm so sorry you haven't met Rolf's brother and sisters, but at least you can come and say goodbye to me and baby Rolf. Come for tea, Rolf usually manages to be home for an hour then.'

They were strolling to the door when Rolf remarked that she wasn't going until Tuesday, was she? Samantha replied suitably and prayed a wordless prayer that Tuesday would never come.

But there was still Sunday; she was called so promptly the next morning that she was dressed and breakfasted and waiting long before Giles arrived, but to start off the day by waiting on the doorstep for him would never do; she retired to her room, and wandered impatiently round it until Jannie the maid came to tell her that the doctor had arrived and was downstairs. Antonia wasn't awake yet, and the Baroness was a late riser, so Samantha went downstairs and met Giles in the hall, answering his friendly good morning in a pleasant voice while her heart drummed against her ribs at the sight of him while she expressed doubt as to what she should do about leaving a message. 'I don't know what time we shall be coming back,' she pointed out. 'If you'll tell me, I'll write a note.'

'No need, I've told Jannie.' He didn't offer to tell her, though, and perhaps it might sound rude if she asked. She accompanied him outside into the peaceful Sunday morning and was ushered into the Merlin.

'You're very silent,' he remarked five minutes later, during which time she had striven to think of a topic of conversation. 'Did you enjoy the dinner party?'

'Yes thank you—I met someone called Henk, he told me why you weren't there.'

'Ah—now I understand this rather frosty manner; you're smitten with compunction because I gave up going to the dinner party in order to spend a day taking you round the sights. Is that it?'

She said snappishly: 'Yes. I would never have come, only Tonia told me that she thought it was a good idea, and she didn't mind.'

His voice was silky. 'That makes everything all right, if Tonia approves?'

'Yes, of course. I'm—I'm very grateful to her.' She added quickly: 'And you too, of course.'

'Of course,' he mocked her gravely. 'And now, having cleared the air of any small differences, I propose that we enjoy ourselves.' He gave her a quick sidelong glance and she saw that he was smiling. 'After all, we have Tonia's blessing.'

She was only too willing to agree; obviously he and Tonia had talked about it and he was, after all, merely giving her a treat before she went back home. The sun, a little reluctant, struggled through the clouds and she said cheerfully, counting it a good omen: 'Oh, look—it's going to be a fine day after all.'

'There's a map in the pocket beside you—we're coming into Groningen now, but we shan't stop. From there we're going to Assen and Meppel and on to Zwolle by a country road, then we'll cross the Veluwe and come out somewhere close to Amersfoort, take a country road again so that you can glimpse Soestdijk Palace, and then on to Hilversum, Amsterdam and finally, Haarlem.' They were going through Groningen now and he paused to point out some of its attractions. 'We'll go back to Dokkum by a much shorter route,' he went on, 'through Alkmaar and over the Afsluitdijk, though it will be dark by then, I'm afraid.'

'It sounds lovely,' commented Samantha, poring over her map, her brain reeling under what sounded like a marathon tour of the Netherlands. 'Isn't that rather a long way?' she ventured.

'No. Holland is small and we have all day.'

All day—it sounded like for ever, and she made up her mind to enjoy every moment of it. With the map open on her knee, she snuggled back in the comfort of her seat and he said at once: 'That's better. Now about this part of the country...'

He was an informative and amusing companion; she learned a great deal as they sped through the wide fields of Friesland and then across the wooded moors of Drente, peaceful and quiet. Giles slowed a little as they neared Meppel, so that she might get a closer look at the occasional pedestrian in the quaint costume of the district, and stopped obligingly in one village because the inhabitants were coming out of church, for a really good view of their charming costumes.

'But don't ask me to take you to Staphorst,' begged her companion, 'it's a pious village and they won't have strangers, let alone cars anywhere near them on a Sunday. Perhaps you remember that there was an outbreak of polio there a year or so ago—they rather set their faces against modern ways and methods, with consequent unhappy results from time to time, but strange though they may seem to the out-side world, I suppose they have as much right to live as they wish as the next man. Now, this next village, Rouveen, has a quite different costume and the people don't mind you look-ing at them.'

He left the main road presently and criss-crossed by narrow lanes over the countryside, not hurrying, so that she could have the leisure to gaze around her. It was some time before they rejoined the motorway again just outside Amersfoort, where Giles obligingly pointed out the Gothic Tower of Our Lady, as well as the Koppelpoort. But they didn't linger; he took the road to Baarn and on past the royal palace, where he stopped for a few minutes before turning into a narrow road alongside it which brought them to an hotel—an old castle, Giles explained, called De Hooge Vuursche. 'Coffee, I think,' he suggested, and led her inside.

It was quiet and very comfortable in the coffee room. Samantha poured out and without quite knowing how, found herself talking about her grandparents and her childhood and Clement's.

'And what do you go back to?' asked Giles.

'I don't know.' She lifted her nice eyes to his and smiled. 'Night duty, I daresay.'

'Have you no choice?'

'Oh, well—perhaps, just a little; I can apply...' She stopped, for she didn't want to boast about her probable appointment as Night Sister, and he said quickly: 'I can understand

that you're not keen to apply for a permanent job.'

She mistook his meaning entirely, unaware
of the mythical Jack who, presumably, would
make a permanent job unnecessary, and agreed
with him cheerfully, looking at his placid face
and wondering what he was thinking behind
all that calm.

They went on again presently, to weave a
way through Hilversum and then Amsterdam.
'You can see very little of it from the car,' he
remarked as she craned her neck to see the roof
tops and churches. 'You need to walk. If we
had more time, we could spend the day roam-
ing the city—some of it is very beautiful.'

Haarlem, when they reached it, was beautiful too and seemed almost as large. The doctor
went slowly now through its older streets,
pointing out the more ancient of the houses as
they went, until finally turning under the arch-
way and stopping in his own courtyard.

As they got out, he asked: 'You won't mind
if I leave you for a few minutes? Klara will be
delighted to look after you and will show you

where to leave your coat. I've a call to make, but it's close by.'

He had opened his house door as he spoke and ushered her inside and across the hall to the same sitting room Samantha had been in before. It was, she decided, as they went in, one of the nicest rooms she had ever seen, with the pale sunshine peering in through the narrow windows and the fire crackling cosily in the vast fireplace. Giles tugged an old-fashioned bellrope and when Klara appeared, took himself off, saying to Samantha that by the time she had tidied herself he would be back. He was as good as his word; she was half way down the staircase as he came through the door again. She could have been quicker, of course, but she had first of all had a short conversation with Juffrouw Boot, largely composed of nods and shakes of the head and smiles, and then, in the charming room to which she had been shown, she had prowled around looking at the portraits on the walls, examining the delicate china, and looking at her own reflection, with great dissatisfaction, in the silver-framed mirror standing on the elegant dressing table. Then she had tidied her hair and powdered her nose and put on a little more lipstick, smoothed down the brown jersey dress and, taking her time, had walked down the gallery lined with more portraits to the stairs. She was deep in a daydream in which she was living in the house—with Giles, of course—and walking down her own staircase, when he came through the little passage into the hall below and stood looking up at her, so that just for a moment of time her dream seemed real and she smiled with fleeting happiness.

As he watched his calm face changed and his grey eyes held a gleam in their depths. He began to walk towards her. 'Samantha,' his voice was quiet and very gentle, 'dear girl...' and stopped, while she, bewildered and out of her dream by now, stared down at him, not certain any more if the look on his face had been a part of it or reality.

Common sense told her that of course it was the former and reminded her that dreaming was a waste of time and could lead to difficulties. She hurried down the last few steps, saying over-brightly: 'Juffrouw Boot and I have had quite a talk, without saying anything much, you know, but it was fun.'

She peeped at him as she reached his side; he returned her look placidly and began to talk about Klara and her burned hands, a subject, with variations, which took them through pre-lunch drinks and well into the soup, and with the coming of the chicken Toque Blanche the doctor switched, with no effort at all, to the more interesting aspects of Haarlem, while Samantha, a little out of her depth in step ga-bles, double steps, St Bavo's mighty organ and the invention of printing, listened a little be-musedly, trying to inspect the room they were in without appearing to do so. It was almost as beautiful as the sitting room, with its pan-elled walls and heavy mahogany furniture of the Empire period which surprisingly enough suited, the old house very well. There was a quantity of silver on display too and still more portraits on the walls; Samantha eyed them with interest and hoped that she was to be taken on a tour of inspection later on, and be-came aware that his eyes were fixed upon her.

'You're not listening,' he accused her, smilingly.

'Oh, I was,' her voice was earnest. 'I do beg your pardon if you think I wasn't—only there is so much to see as well as listen to, and I'm so afraid of missing something.'

She gave him an apologetic smile across the table; any other man might have taken offence, but she could see that he had understood, and loved him a little more for it. She embarked on the soufflé, a thing as light as air, and when she remarked upon it he laughed at her again. 'I have an excellent cook, Klara runs the house and does the housekeeping, but Ria reigns in the kitchen.' He leaned back in his chair, still smiling a little. 'There is a girl too, Corrie, who does the housework, and Mevrouw Plat who comes in each day to help.'

Samantha's eyes had become round. 'So many?' she commented. 'It must be a very large house.'

'Very,' he agreed gravely. 'If you have finished, we will have our coffee in the sitting room and presently, if you wish, I will take you round.'

The house was indeed large, although a number of its rooms were surprisingly small. Samantha, happily peering into them as he obligingly threw open their doors, remarked upon this. 'Why,' she exclaimed, 'there are so many rooms you surely don't use half of them from one year's end to the next.'

'I don't, but I know every stick of furniture in them, and Klara sees to it that they are opened up regularly and polished and cleaned and aired. You see, the house has hardly changed since it was built centuries ago, although it has been added to and modernised and I like to keep it that way, although I admit it is too big for me.' He added: 'At present.'

She had her back to him, examining a dear little worktable. 'But when you marry you will be able to open up some of the rooms at least.'

'Indeed I shall. This place was built in the days of large families, and while I don't expect to father a dozen children, I should certainly hope for a sizeable family.'

She turned round at that and said impulsively: 'Oh, yes, it's a house made for children, isn't it? All these lovely crooked passages and little rooms.'

Giles was leaning against a wall, watching her. 'Your interest in my future flatters me,' he remarked blandly. 'Such a pity that you will never know.'

She turned her back on him and bent to examine the work-table once again, seeking desperately for another topic of conversation; she didn't want to know what happened to him once she had left Holland, she told herself fiercely—let him marry and settle down and have a bunch of horrid little boys with black eyebrows and grey eyes. She heard him say, half laughing, 'If you don't come away from that work table soon, I shall feel that I must make you a present of it. Come and see the drawing room—I left it until last because it's a little surprising.'

It was at the back of the house, with a great bay window reaching from floor to ceiling and overlooking a small paved courtyard, and large enough to take fifty people in the greatest comfort, and yet, despite its size, it was quite beautiful and comfortable too, with a great many easy-chairs and tables scattered about, enormous pillow cupboards against its tapestry-covered walls, and a noble hearth flanked by two large chesterfields covered in the wine-coloured velvet of the curtains. Samantha paused in the doorway, as surprised as her companion had predicted, and then started on a tour of inspection. 'It's super,' she told him, 'simply super, and lived-in too—do you hold parties here?'

'Occasionally, and I use it frequently when I have friends in for dinner or drinks. It hasn't been changed for a long time and I wouldn't want it different.'

'I should think not,' agreed Samantha. 'All the same, it rather takes one's breath away,' she was trying out a small buttoned crinoline chair by the window. 'It's so very large and tucked away.' She got up again reluctantly. 'Thank you for showing me your home. I can understand why you love it so much—I shall have a lot to tell Grandmother when I see her.'

They were strolling, side by side, to the door. 'How are you travelling?' he wanted to know.

'I'm to fly. Baron van Duyren got my ticket yesterday. He's driving me to Schiphol. I shall be in London by teatime.'

She hoped her voice sounded cheerful and apparently it did, for all he said was: 'And on duty the next day, I suppose.'

She laughed. 'Of course.' It didn't bear thinking about and she changed the conversation. 'I've seen your cat and her kittens—Klara showed them to me, but haven't you a dog?'

'He died a month ago. He was very old and I miss him greatly.'

Her sympathy was warm and immediate. 'Oh, I know how you feel. I'm sorry. You should get a puppy as soon as you can, you know. It sounds heartless, but really it's a compliment to your dog.'

'What kind of puppy should I get?'

She considered. 'Something large and good-natured—a golden Labrador, I think; they're family dogs. What did you have?'

'An Alsatian. I called him King.'

She said in a soft voice: 'Oh, poor Giles—they become such good friends, don't they? You could call the puppy Prince.'

'Would you like that? Then a golden Labrador called Prince it shall be.'

'That's nice of you, but I won't know, will I?' she reminded him. 'But I should like to think that you…' She paused, in difficulties, and he asked: 'That I what?'

'Had another dog,' she finished lamely.

They had tea round the sitting room fire before he showed her his study and the small consulting room leading from it where he saw his private patients. 'I've rooms in the city, of course, but sometimes it is more convenient if the patients come here.'

'You have a large practice?'

'Yes—too large. I shall have to think about taking a partner—it would give me more freedom too.'

He would need that if he married Antonia, reflected Samantha, and asked him if he wished to take her back to Dokkum before the evening got too old.

His voice was silky. 'Why? Are you bored?'

'No,' she was so indignant she could hardly get the word out, 'of course I'm not—what a ridiculous thing to say, only you might have plans for the evening and I wouldn't want to interfere with them.'

'I have got plans,' he smiled at her. 'We're going to have dinner in Bolsward, just the other side of the Afsluitdijk, and you will certainly interfere with my plans if you refuse to come.'

It was her turn to smile, looking unexpectedly pretty in the soft lamplight. 'I'd like that very much.'

'Good, and now that point is dealt with, let us sit and talk without you starting up every few minutes with some mistaken idea or other.'

It was the happiest hour that she had spent for a long time, Samantha admitted to herself afterwards. They didn't talk about themselves, but they had a great deal in common, she discovered before very long; she hadn't said half of what she wanted to say when Giles remarked regretfully:

'I'm sorry we can't go on like this for hours, but we must make a move if we are to reach Bolsward in time for dinner.'

So she fetched her things and had another little chat with Juffrouw Boot before bidding her goodbye and went out with Giles to where the car was waiting in the courtyard, and presently, when they were well on their way, they began to talk again.

The restaurant in Bolsward was pleasant and the food delicious. They lingered over it until Samantha happened to glance at her watch and saw with horror that it was already eleven o'clock.

There was no one about when they reached the house in Dokkum but the door yielded to Giles' hand on its great brass knob and he followed her into the hall, where she embarked on a speech of thanks for her delightful day which he brought to an abrupt halt by taking her in his arms and kissing her.

'It was my delightful day too,' he told her. 'Good night, enchanting Samantha.'

She drew away from his arms. 'Goodbye, Giles.' It was an effort to keep her voice light.

'I never say goodbye,' he replied, and went to the door. 'Lock this behind me, dear girl.'

She bolted and locked the door, hardly seeing the key, for the tears in her eyes; she was locking him out of her life, wasn't she? She listened to the gentle swish of the Merlin's tyres getting fainter and when there was silence she went up to bed.

CHAPTER EIGHT

MONDAY WAS a day to be got through some-how, Samantha discovered. Now that she had seen Giles for the last time she wished with all her heart to be gone—back to London and the hospital and hard work so that she would have very little time to think about him.

She had got up heavy-eyed, after an almost sleepless night, eaten her breakfast with Antonia and had had a talk with the Baroness before going back to her own room to do a little packing, and after their morning coffee, when Antonia suddenly remembered that she should pay her dentist a visit, Samantha was only too glad to get out the car and drive her erstwhile patient into Gronigen. It was a cold, grey morning, as cold and grey as Samantha felt, and the effort to match her companion's high spirits was almost more than she could manage, especially when Antonia fell to dis-cussing her outing with Giles.

'He's such a dear,' she informed Samantha, just as though she didn't know that for herself. 'I've known him since I was a baby, did you know? He was there when I was christened. And did you not like his house, Sam? Rolf has a nice house too, but I like the house of Giles better.'

Samantha, her nerves decidedly on edge, murmured a nothing and applied herself to her driving.

'He has a dear old grandmother,' continued Antonia chattily. 'She will not live with him, for she has a house by the sea at Zandvoort, with plenty of servants and an old dragon of a—a companion—is that the right word? And his brothers are in Canada, but not for ever; they are scientists and still young: Sometimes they come to pay Giles a visit and sometimes he goes to Canada to see them; he is so much the elder, you see. If he were not so very busy he would be lonely, but then he has a great many friends too.'

Samantha couldn't resist the temptation of saying: 'Well, he doesn't need to be lonely. He can always get married.'

Antonia nodded. 'Oh, yes—and he will make a splendid husband, Sam, for he always knows what to do,' an artless point of view which Samantha found touching. 'He has a great deal of money, too.' Antonia turned to smile at her, her pretty face very engaging. 'I have money too—Rolf looks after it for me.'

'How nice,' uttered Samantha inadequately and hurried the little car past a truck and trailer. She drove well, but driving on the wrong side of the road made her nervous, and besides, she couldn't bear to talk about Giles any longer. She said quickly before Antonia could begin again: 'Did you see that pigskin suit in *Harper and Queen*'s—it would be awfully useful for this time of year.'

Antonia was instantly diverted. 'Yes—think I shall order it from Simpson's, or perhaps I might go over to London and get it. And you, Sam dear? You will buy it too?'

A month's salary, calculated Samantha, and if she bought it she wouldn't be able to pay any rent, neither would she be able to eat or drink and certainly not go home for her days off. She said mildly: 'I don't think so—I shouldn't get enough wear out of it.'

'You are probably right.' agreed her companion seriously, 'for you are always in your hospital uniform—although it is a pretty uniform,' she conceded kindly, 'and in your cape and funny little bonnet you look so *deftig*,' she frowned over the translation. 'This is respectable, or perhaps dignified is better…'

Samantha turned the car neatly into the narrow street which would take them over the canal into Dokkum. 'I'm flattered,' she said dryly. Was that how Giles thought of her? she wondered—not that it mattered any more. She inched the car down the lane leading to the house, suddenly glad that the trip was over.

But the remainder of the day turned out to be almost as bad; at lunch Antonia and her mother held a lively discussion as to whether Giles had promised to take Antonia to Haarlem the following weekend or not. 'He told me,' stated Antonia positively, 'that he had to go somewhere or other, I no longer remember where.' She pouted a little. 'If he is not free,

I shall drive myself down and go to the hospital.'

'You can't do that,' her mother told her sharply, and Antonia appealed to Samantha, pecking at her food and looking a little pale. 'Did he tell you, Sam?'

Samantha replied that no, he hadn't, repressing a desire to point out that Giles was hardly likely to confide in her when it concerned his private life. It was a relief when the talk centred round the wedding of some friend of Antonia's.

They all went over to Rolf's for tea; a pleasant informal meal and very English with the large tea-tray and silver teapot, and plates of tiny sandwiches and fingers of buttered toast. They sat round the fire, with baby Rolf, plump and solemn, on his father's knee, and the talk was comfortably of babies and small family matters and Samantha's future at the hospital. No one mentioned Giles, and Samantha, with the contrariness of those in love, was quite put out. It was Sappha who said, as they were taking their leave: 'I'll not say goodbye, Samantha, for I'm sure we shall meet again.'

She had kissed her warmly and Rolf had taken her hand and stared at her rather disconcertingly.

'Sorry to be leaving us?' he wanted to know kindly.

Samantha nodded. 'Yes, oh, yes, I—well, it's been...' She stopped, and he filled the awkward gap for her.

'I too have every hope that we shall meet again,' he told her, and because she had glanced down to Charlie the Alsatian who had wormed his way between them, she didn't see the Baron's swift, bright glance at his wife and the tiny answering smile on her face.

The Baron came for her early, after breakfast the next morning, and because she had already said her goodbyes, she didn't keep him waiting but got into the car beside him and was whisked away with barely time to wave to the little group gathered on the doorstep to see her off.

'Sensible girl,' he remarked approvingly. 'Goodbyes are difficult, aren't they? Either they shouldn't be said or said quickly. Tell me, do you go straight to Clement's when you arrive in London?'

By the time Samantha had outlined her plans to him they were almost at the Afsluitdijk, and he went on to talk about nothing in particular in a pleasant manner which had the effect of taking her mind off her thoughts. It was as they were approaching the sluice at its end that he remarked casually: 'It quite slipped my mind—I'm taking you as far as Haarlem and handing you over to Giles. An unexpected meeting I have to attend in a couple of hours. He is free, luckily, and has no objection to taking you on to Schiphol.' He glanced at her briefly. 'I knew you would understand and not mind, although I apologize for not taking you the whole way.'

The wide grey sky flashing past the car's windows didn't seem grey any more; she had to wait a minute before she answered in case he should hear the delight in her voice. 'I don't mind a bit,' she said at length with calm. 'It's very kind of you to take the trouble to drive me at all. Giles won't mind?'

'No, he won't mind.' They were tearing down the road towards Alkmaar now and presently through its bustling centre, to pick up speed once more when they were clear of it and on the highway to Haarlem.

They got there a little early; Giles was seeing a patient in his study when they were admitted by Klara, who led them to the sitting room and reappeared within a few minutes with the coffee tray. They had had one cup and Samantha was pouring out a second cup for each of them when Giles came into the room. And if she had cherished secret hopes of his showing delight at seeing her again, she was doomed to disappointment; he greeted her pleasantly but with a casual air which forced her to ask him immediately if he found it annoying to drive her the rest of the way to the airport.

'My dear Sam,' he told her blandly, 'you know me well enough by now to realize that I never do things I don't wish to do. I am delighted to take you.' He gave her a quizzical look. 'I didn't know that we had quarrelled since we last met.'

She went a bright pink, thankful that the Baron, having disposed of his coffee, was stretched out in his chair with his eyes shut.

'Don't be ridiculous,' she said, a thought waspish. 'Only we've said goodbye…'

'You did. I can distinctly remember telling you that I never say goodbye,' he reminded her silkily. 'You can see now how wise a rule that is; I can think of nothing worse than a mawkish leavetaking, only to meet again within a few hours.'

Samantha remained silent, not sure if he was accusing her of having been mawkish, and when he suggested that they should be on their way, she got to her feet at once, as did the Baron, who had opened his eyes at the remark and, apparently much refreshed, made his farewells with a swiftness which bore out his previous remarks, got into his car and drove off, leaving Giles to put Samantha's cases into the boot of the Merlin, shrug himself into his coat, open the door for her to get in and then get in himself.

She glanced at her watch as he slid the car under the arch into the street and began to make his way through Haarlem towards the motorway. There was plenty of time, she thought, but perhaps the traffic was heavy. Presumably he knew at what time her plane left.

He was silent, and for something to say she uttered the first thing which came into her head. 'It's very kind of you to drive me all this way.'

'Twenty kilometres, and I am kind.' A remark which effectively caused her silence for five minutes or more, but presently, on the motorway, eating up the flat road ahead of them, she broke a stillness which had become intolerable to her. 'It's not a very nice day,' she said, and when she got no answer, 'I expect you want to get back to your surgery.'

'Not particularly. I've seen my patients for the morning, there will be time enough to do the visits before lunch.'

She was racking her brains to find a fresh topic of conversation when Giles slowed the car and turned off the motorway on one of its outlets. It took them to a quiet, straight country road leading to the flat green fields stretching away before them.

'Is this the way?' she asked.

'No, but we have time to spare.' He stopped the car by the side of the road and turned to look at her. 'Do you want to go back to England, Sam?'

She said at once: 'Of course,' and wondered miserably why she should have to tell him a lie when she longed to say how much she wanted to stay. But then he might want to know why—and there was still Antonia. Samantha knew now, deep in her bones, that he liked her; if she had been clever and unscrupulous and pretty besides, she would have known what to do, but she was none of these things, and over and above that Giles and Antonia had known each other for years and it was only a few short weeks since she and Giles had met.

'You have your plans for the future?' His voice was pleasant but impersonal.

'Oh, yes—it's quite settled, and—and being away has made me even more certain.'

'So I must say again "Absence makes the heart grow fonder," mustn't I?'

'Something like that.' It seemed a strange way to describe her feelings about the new job she knew now she would accept, but it would do as well as any. She said carefully: 'It's nice to have it all settled.'

'You have quite made up your mind?'

'Yes, oh, yes.' She spoke quickly with false enthusiasm, swallowing back the words she wanted to say.

Giles nodded his handsome head. 'Ah, well—we'll leave it for the moment.' His voice was mild. 'I'm a patient man, I've learned to wait for what I want.'

He had been waiting for Antonia, hadn't he, and perhaps he would still have to wait, because she was very young and even if she loved him, she might not want to settle down just yet. 'I hope you get it,' she spoke politely and then, suddenly wanting to be gone, away from Holland and him, she added urgently: 'Ought we to go?'

He drove on at once, circling round the motorway and joining it again after a mile or so.

They reached Schiphol with too much time in hand and spent half an hour over coffee, talking about nothing that mattered until Samantha's flight was called. He walked with her as far as he was allowed to go and then stopped to take her hands in his. 'I have to go away for a few days,' he told her. 'I hope that when I return there will be news from you.' He bent his head and kissed her slowly and she said in a voice muffled with tears: 'Oh, Giles—goodbye.'

He let her go. 'I never say goodbye. Remember?'

She had read somewhere that strong emotions emptied one of all feeling; it was quite true, she now discovered. She sat staring out of the porthole at the mass of cloud below and about the plane and felt nothing at all; she was in a mental limbo from which she had no doubt she would presently emerge, back into a painful world, but for the present she was quite unable to believe that she would never see Giles again, nor could she envisage a future without him.

Her mind was still numb when she reached Clement's. She reported at the office, answered the Office Sister's questions politely, accepted the unwelcome news that she was to spend the next few days doing holiday duties round the hospital, and on being dismissed, walked round to the flat with her luggage. There was no one there; her three friends were on duty; indeed, the whole house seemed empty, only old Mr Cockburn waved happily to her from his window as she climbed the steps to the front door.

The flat looked cold and unwelcoming and the washing-up from breakfast hadn't been done. Samantha put her bags in her room, disposed of the cups and saucers and plates and then put on the kettle and made herself a cup of tea. She supposed that presently she ought to see about something for their suppers, quite overlooking the fact that she had eaten nothing since breakfast that morning, for the tray of coffee and sandwiches which she had been offered on the plane she had left untouched; she hadn't felt hungry, she wasn't hungry now, but the tea was hot and comforting.

She had bestirred herself to unpack, get her uniform ready for the next day, and make a Quiche Lorraine for supper before her friends returned. They greeted her with cries of pleasure and a great deal of disjointed talk. Sue had become engaged only two days previously, she was told by all three at once; Joan had been offered a post with a good future at the country branch of Clement's which dealt exclusively with children. Only Pam was left, as they pointed out to Samantha, because she herself would naturally get the post of Night Sister, wouldn't she?

'I suppose so,' said Samantha without enthusiasm, so that Pam said at once: 'Don't tell us that your trip abroad has filled your head with ideas? Or is it that handsome charmer who called round to see you—that morning you went to the launderette. He wanted to know where you were because he had something to say to you and he was on the point of leaving England within the hour, or something equally dramatic, remember? All very high-handed,' she giggled cheerfully, 'and do you know what I told him, Sam? That you'd gone off for the day with Jack, and when he said ''Who is Jack?'' I told him it was the man you were engaged to.'

Samantha felt the colour drain from her face; a dozen memories of things Giles had said to her in Holland rushed helter-skelter into her mind. Now she understood; he hadn't been talking about her job at all but about her future with the mythical Jack. She asked through stiff lips: 'Was he surprised?'

'Well, ducky,' commented Pam carelessly, 'he's the type to keep his feelings well tucked away behind that handsome face, isn't he? He muttered something polite about going on his way. And a good thing too, Sam—we all thought he was chatting you up, and you're such an innocent.'

Samantha smiled, although it was a great effort to do so, and when Joan remarked on her pallor, mentioned, with no truth whatever, that the flight hadn't agreed with her and if they didn't mind she thought she would go to bed with a couple of Panadol and a hot drink, but even when they had fussed around her, filling her hot water bottle and making tea and at last leaving her alone, she couldn't sleep. She lay for most of the night, staring into the dark, trying to decide whether to write to Giles and tell him that there was no Jack, no anyone...

She whiled away the long hours composing a letter to him in her head, only to decide that to write would be an impossibility because of Antonia; nothing had altered really; he would still marry Antonia, and since he thought her own future was settled, he would probably forget all about her. It was a silly situation, she told herself sternly, and one which she would have to accept with as good a grace as she was able. On this high-minded thought she closed her aching, puffy eyes and went to sleep.

The next day was horrible; she was sent to Men's Medical because the staff nurse there was off sick with a sore throat. Samantha loathed medical nursing and Sister Thwaites was a tiresome, middle-aged woman, forever stating the obvious and preventing the nurses from finishing their work, for she had a genius for ordering them to start something else when they had only half done. The ward was not a happy one, and to add to Samantha's ill-humour, she was given a split duty—not really allowed—which meant going to second dinner and returning to the ward at five o'clock. She went back to the flat, not bothering to go down for a meal, made herself some coffee, tidied up and then sat down to write a letter to Antonia. She wrote to the Baroness too, and then to Sappha, and posted them on her way back to the hospital. She thought it unlikely that she would get a reply; she had been in Dokkum for such a short period and she was unlikely to meet any of them again, however kindly they had hoped to the contrary—besides, she knew from her years in hospital that once people were well again they tended, naturally enough, to forget the nurses on whom they had depended, sometimes for their very lives, a fact she didn't resent in the least.

Hurrying back to go on duty, she resolved to telephone her grandparents that evening; she had written to them from Dokkum; now she was filled with a longing to see them and the little cottage at Langton Herring, although even there, there would be memories of Giles—it was going to be difficult to escape him, but escape him she would, she told herself stoutly as she opened the office door where Sister Thwaites was waiting to give her the report.

Three days later there was a letter from Antonia. Samantha collected it when she went down for coffee. There was one from her grandmother too, and she read that first, and then, because she got involved in some discussion or other with some of the other staff nurses, there was no time to read the letter from Holland. It burned a hole in her pocket until, most fortunately, Sister asked her to go and test all the specimens again, because the student nurse who had already done them wasn't to be trusted, according to Sister Thwaites, and it was Doctor Duggan's round in another hour's time.

Samantha made short work of her task. She reckoned she could spare five minutes to read her letter; no one was likely to bother her in the tiny cupboardlike room where such work was done. She took it from her pocket and opened it. It wasn't a long letter. In it, after an impassioned opening deploring Samantha's absence, Antonia had written that she was to be married—quite soon. She would have told her dear Sam when she had been in Dokkum, but it hadn't been official and anyway she would have guessed, and how wonderful it was that Sam had got on so well with the man she was to marry and of course—heavily under-lined—she was to attend the wedding.

Samantha drew a difficult breath and read the letter again—it was there, in black and white, and even though she had known it, it was a shock which made her feel sick. Her eye skimmed over the last few lines, given over to ecstatic comments about wedding clothes, a subject dear to Antonia's heart, and a state-ment to the effect that she was always Samantha's very affectionate friend.

Samantha folded the letter with great care, as though that were of great importance, and put it carefully back into her pocket, then she picked up the neatly written results of her tests and went back into the ward, where she handed them to Sister Thwaites. In the brief time it had taken her to walk down the ward she had made up her mind about something. She said now: 'Sister, I should like to go to Matron's office now. There's something urgent I have to see her about.'

Sister Thwaites frowned. 'Doctor Duggan will be here in half an hour,' she pointed out grumblingly, 'but I suppose if Matron wishes to see you you'll have to go. But you're to come straight back.'

The Office Sister who guarded Matron from chance callers wasn't disposed to listen to Samantha. 'You must make an appointment, Staff Nurse, like everyone else,' she said crossly. 'Tomorrow morning…'

'Now,' said Samantha, 'if you please, Sister.'

The older woman stared at her and then lifted the receiver of the house telephone. She looked crosser than ever when she put it down. 'You can go in,' she snapped.

Samantha, once inside, wasted no time. To her request to leave Clement's at the earliest possible moment, Matron raised neatly plucked eyebrows, only contenting herself with asking, quite nicely, why Samantha should wish to go just as the future held such promise for her. 'And you such a level-headed girl,' commented Matron, allowing herself to show surprise, 'for you do realize, Staff Nurse, that you would have been given the post of Junior Night Sister?'

'It's a personal matter, Matron,' said Samantha, more clear in the head than she had been for days. 'I have three weeks' holiday due to me and no sick leave to make up—if I could save my days off, I could leave in three days' time.'

Matron gave her a considered look. 'And if I should refuse your request, Staff Nurse?'

'I'm afraid that I should just go, Matron. I don't quite know what would happen if I did, but it really doesn't matter.'

'You're not in any trouble?'

'No, Matron.'

'In that case and since you're determined, I must allow you to leave. I'm very sorry that you should wish to do so and I hope that you will never regret it.' Matron nodded briskly. 'You may go in three days' time, Staff Nurse. I will see that the General Office knows about it so that you can collect your money and cards then.' She lowered her capped head over the papers before her and Samantha, recognising dismissal, went.

She broke the news to her friends that evening after they had eaten their supper, a sustaining one of fried eggs and chips, washed down with quantities of tea. And there was an immediate outcry of: 'You can't, Sam—you're throwing away a marvellous job. Think of the lolly—and the darling little cap you'll wear.' They stared at her, openmouthed with surprise.

'I want a change,' said Samantha, calm with despair; if her future was to be in ruins, then she would at least choose those ruins for herself. 'There's a super job going in Brazil,' she took no notice of her companions' incredulous faces, 'some mining firm or other want a Nursing Sister—there's a good salary and a free flat and...'

'Sam,' it was Joan speaking, 'you'd hate it, and you'll be miles away from everyone.'

Samantha examined a delicate pink nail—and wasn't that what she wanted, to get away from everyone—and wasn't Giles everyone? 'I shan't mind,' she said simply. 'I've already written and applied for it.'

She glanced up at the three anxious faces. 'It's all right about the flat, isn't it? We're all going away, aren't we, excepting Pam.'

That young lady grinned. 'Don't worry about me. I've not mentioned it before, but I'm thinking of getting married myself—I had planned to leave in about three months, but since we're all set on doing our own thing as soon as possible, I can just as well give in my notice.'

'Poor Matron,' remarked Joan.

'Yes—where will she ever find four such splendid nurses as we are?' put in Pam flippantly. 'Sam, have you really made up your mind about this job in Brazil?'

Samantha started collecting the supper dishes from the table. 'Yes, I think it sounds great.' She felt pleased with her voice—gay and light, the antithesis of the leaden heart under her ribs.

'Did you see much of the charmer while you were in Holland?' Pam enquired idly as she followed Samantha into the kitchen.

Samantha's voice was still miraculously light. 'Oh, now and then, you know. He—he came up to see Antonia.'

'Huh, I suppose he drove a Rolls-Royce and lived in a mansion.'

'As a matter of fact, he did. Look, ought we to go down and see Cocky?' She walked to the sink and turned on the tap. 'We've paid the rent until the end of the month, haven't we?'

It was a red herring of exactly the right kind to divert everyone's attention away from herself. Pam and Sue volunteered to go down to the basement flat while she and Joan washed up. They were back long before the dishes were dry with the news that although Cocky was sorry to see them go he had no fears about re-letting the flat at once; there was always a queue for a home, even such a humble one as theirs.

The question of their futures having been satisfactorily settled, a final cup of coffee was called for before the four of them began to wrangle mildly as to who should have the bath first. In the end they tossed up and Samantha won, and Pam, studying her under the glare of the Woolworth plastic light shade, gave it her opinion that it was a good thing that she had. 'You look as though you could do with a nice relaxing bath, Sam,' she pronounced. 'You're positively lined and wrinkled, and I swear you've lost weight. Didn't they feed you?'

Samantha thought back into that other world she wasn't going to see again. 'Yes, the food was marvellous—absolutely super.'

Joan was on her way to her room, but she turned back to ask: 'Did you go out at all, Sam?'

'Yes.'

'Well, let's hear. Where and who with?'

'Well, to Baron van Duyren's house, one of those large…'

'Yes, yes, we know…where else did you go?'

It was like turning a knife in a wound. 'I went to Doctor ter Ossel's house—to see Juffrouw Boot.'

'Naturally.' It was Pam speaking. 'Did you spend the day with her?'

'No, of course not. I—we went over the house.'

'Who's we?' chorused her friends. 'And why have you been holding out on us—you've been back days…'

Samantha ignored that. 'Doctor ter Ossel and me. It's a lovely old house with a great many rooms.' Her face was stiff with the smile she had pinned upon it. She could have hugged Sue when she cried: 'For heaven's sake, we're all on duty in the morning, we'll never be up. Are you still on Men's Medical, Sam?'

Samantha was making for the bathroom. 'Yes, for my sins. I expect I shall be there until I leave.'

She was right, but it didn't matter, nothing mattered much any more. She went through the days, working too hard, trying to tire herself out so that she would sleep when she went to bed, but she seemed, for the time being at least, beyond sleep. She lay and thought about Giles and remembered everything that he had said, and wondered for the hundredth time if things would have been different if he had known that she wasn't engaged, nor likely to be. And although each night common sense told her that she was a fool to go on thinking about him, it made no difference at all, so that by the last day at Clement's she had black shadows under her eyes and a colourless face which looked more ordinary than ever, besides being dreadfully short-tempered from lack of sleep.

She wished everyone goodbye, expressed suitable gratitude to those of her friends who had pressed parting gifts upon her and got herself and her various bits of luggage into a taxi for Waterloo Station and the train for Weymouth. She had written to her grandparents and had received a letter back—a kind letter over which she had wept a little, because it was apparent from it that they were puzzled and upset but far too considerate of her feelings to ask questions. They had even accepted her plan to go to Brazil, although they must have thought her very selfish to have made such a decision—she would have to do her best to explain when she saw them.

She opened the paper she had brought and then dropped it on her lap to look out of the window. Giles would be in his lovely home, seeing his patients. 'Fool,' she said, quite loudly, forgetting where she was, and looked up to encounter the surprised stares of two ladies sitting opposite her. They were respectable matrons, wearing the right clothes and good imitation pearls; she half smiled at them, but the stares became cold, so she turned to the window again, wondering stupidly if Giles had stopped for his coffee or whether he waited until he had finished seeing his patients. She closed her eyes to see him the more clearly beneath their lids. He would be drinking his coffee, she decided.

He was doing nothing of the kind; he was in Dokkum, sitting in Baroness van Duyren's sitting room, talking to Antonia and her mother.

'You say you wrote to her, Tonia—how long ago?' he wanted to know.

'Five—six days. I invited her to my wedding. I told her I was going to be married—I cannot understand... Perhaps she is upset because I said nothing while she was here. I shall telephone...'

Giles said sharply: 'No—I'll deal with it.' He frowned. 'It seems strange.'

'What seems strange?' Sappha had walked in to join them.

'I was telling Giles about Sam,' explained Antonia. 'She would not be so unkind as not to write to me? I have had but one little note.'

Sappha shook her head. 'Heavens, no—she's the sweetest creature, she wouldn't hurt anyone. She might be busy, though; remember she was going to take up this new job—there would be uniform fittings and forms to fill in and so on and probably straight back on night duty after her first day or two.'

'What new job?' Giles's voice was very quiet.

Sappha looked startled. 'Didn't you know? She was offered the post of Night Sister before she came here, but she hadn't made up her mind, but something decided her while she was with Tonia.'

Giles had got up and was standing with his back to the room, looking out of the window. 'I was under the impression that she was going to get married.' He added harshly: 'His name is Jack.'

'Bah,' said Sappha roundly, 'someone was having you on. Why, she told me about this job soon after she got here and said that if she could hang on to it she might get promoted to Senior Night Sister, and when I asked her if that was what she wanted she said she hadn't much choice. I even asked her if she didn't want to marry and she said that she thought it unlikely that anyone would want to ask her—you see, she thinks she's plain and rather dull.' Sappha crossed the room and went to stand by Giles. 'You didn't know,' she stated softly.

'No. But I know now.' He smiled down at her, his face rather pale and set. 'I wonder why she allowed me to think that?'

'I don't know, but now I know why you didn't…' She stopped, smiling. 'Rolf would tell me to mind my own business, but she's so right for you, Giles.' She paused, deep in thought. 'I wonder… Tonia, did you say to whom you were to be married when you wrote to Sam?'

Antonia crossed the room to join them. 'No, but she met Henk at your dinner party—she must have known.'

'How could she, if no one had told her? But you and Giles—he took you down to Haarlem to see Henk, didn't he? and he came to see you when you were in Clement's and…' She looked at Giles, who for once looked startled.

'But how could she think—it's ridiculous; Tonia's half my age—good lord, I've known her since she was born; she's a kind of little sister…' He broke off. 'If it had been you, Sappha, what would you have thought?'

She gave him an almost motherly look. 'Just what Samantha thought, and is still thinking. You see? How could she have known?'

He grinned suddenly, then glanced at his watch. 'You won't mind if I leave you?' and went to make his excuses to the Baroness.

He was in London that evening, quite late, having caught the car ferry by the skin of his teeth and skimmed up the motorway from Dover at a steady seventy miles an hour. He parked the car outside the flat and mounted the steps, not forgetting to raise a hand in greeting to old Mr Cockburn, still peering from his window, even at that late hour. There were still lights showing on the top floor and he rang the bell; he would have rung it just the same if the place had been in darkness. Now he waited patiently, listening to shuffling feet and voices raised in argument as to who should go to the door. It was Joan who opened the door, dressing-gowned and hair-netted for bed. She looked at him in silence, nodded to his civil good evening, said surprisingly: 'It's you. I'm glad you've come, but Sam's not here.' She opened the door a little wider. 'You'd better come in.'

There was no one in the sitting room, but when Joan called: 'Pam, Sue, come in here,' they appeared, clutching dressing gowns around them, their heads inevitably crowned with curlers. Giles, apparently unmoved by their homely appearance, wished them a good evening too. 'I apologize for calling at this hour,' he said pleasantly. 'I won't keep you. It is you I wanted to see.' He looked at Pam. 'Tell me, is Sam going to marry—er—Jack, I believe the name was?'

'Why do you want to know?' asked Pam.

'I want to marry her myself.' He smiled. 'You will appreciate that it will help to clear up the situation if I knew the truth.'

Pam swallowed. 'Look, there's no Jack,' she told him. 'I'm sorry I ever said it, only we thought you were just chatting Sam up, and she's such a dear and she doesn't know much about men. We did it for the best.'

He said with no trace of ill-humour: 'I'm sure you did. Will you tell me where she is?'

'She's left Clement's. She's gone home to Langton Herring.'

He moved to the door. 'Thank you. I'll bid you all a good night.'

They all went with him. 'She's got some ridiculous ideas about what she's going to do,' warned Pam.

He turned at the doorway. 'Then I must change her mind for her, must I not?' He included all three of them in a warm smile and was gone before any of them thought of asking him what he intended doing next. He probably wouldn't have told them anyway, although he knew exactly what he needed to do before he could travel down to Dorset and claim his

Samantha. It was irksome to him that he would have to delay his journey, even for a few hours, but as he had said, he was a man of patience; he would need the whole of the day to make his arrangements, but he could travel down very early on the following morning. He bent his powerful mind to achieving his purpose as he drove away.

CHAPTER NINE

SAMANTHA FOUND IT much harder to explain to her grandparents than she had thought possible, partly because the affection they had for her was so great that they were prepared to accept anything she might suggest. It had been difficult, too, to avoid talking too much about Giles and even more difficult giving her reasons for wishing to go to the other side of the world to work when there was a perfectly good job waiting for her in London.

Her grandmother had said wistfully, as they sat together after lunch, 'I suppose this work in Brazil will be exciting, darling, and I'm sure you'll want a change after so many years at Clement's. Is it for a long time?'

'A year, Granny, but the salary's terrific, and when I leave I shall get two months' paid holiday.'

Her grandmother crocheted a row in silence, then: 'That will be nice, Sam dear, and of course you must do what you want; you know that your grandfather and I will agree to whatever you decide.'

Samantha had Stubbs on her lap. She stroked his plump back and said: 'Yes, Granny, I know, and thank you both.'

The silence stretched, taut as elastic, until Mrs Fielding asked:

'You don't feel you can tell us, darling—the reason why you want to go so far away? Is it something to do with that nice Doctor ter Ossel?'

'Yes,' said Samantha baldly.

The old lady allowed a relieved sigh to escape her. 'Well, I'm sure he'll put right whatever is wrong,' she observed.

'No,' said Samantha slowly, 'he can't, Granny. He and Antonia are going to be married. I had a letter from her inviting me to the wedding.'

'Yes, dear, I daresay you did,' persisted her grandparent. 'It's surprising how these mistakes occur, and they're almost always put right before any great harm is done.'

Samantha had no answer to this fanciful remark. She thought with loving tolerance that her grandparents weren't as young as they were; the elderly sometimes had strange ideas and had every right to indulge them should they so wish. She put the indignant Stubbs on the floor and went to get the tea.

Mrs Humphries-Potter came in after tea for one of her little chats, which really meant that she sat sipping a glass of Mrs Fielding's elderberry wine and firing questions at Samantha—awkward questions which made her reasons for leaving Clement's sound silly and her wish to go to Brazil even sillier. Having extracted all the information she could about this, Mrs Humphries-Potter turned to fresh fields.

'And Holland?' she wanted to know. 'Did you enjoy your stay there, Samantha?'

Samantha replied that yes, she had. She enlarged upon this by adding that the country was quite pretty though flat, that the houses were picturesque and some of the cities were modern in parts and that the people she had met had been very kind to her. This last was a mistake, she knew it the moment she had uttered, for her questioner immediately wanted to know if she had seen Giles ter Ossel.

'Yes,' said Samantha, 'from time to time.'

Mrs Humphries-Potter was like a dog with a fresh, meaty bone. She leaned forward in her chair. 'Tell me all about him, child.'

Samantha shot her grandmother a lightning, imploring look, and that astute lady said instantly: 'Yes, do tell about his house, Samantha, for Mrs Humphries-Potter shares my interest in antiques, don't you?' she appealed to her guest. 'There's some interesting silver…'

So Samantha, thankfully taking her cue, spent a feverish half hour talking about silver-gilt in the rococo style, silver wall sconces in the style of baroque and some splendid furniture mounts dating from the early eighteenth century. She knew only a little upon these subjects, so she spun their descriptions out for as long as possible, and even then was forced to repeat herself. But her purpose was served; Mrs Humphries-Potter, her mind quite diverted from Samantha and her doings in Holland, got up to go at last, still talking knowledgeably about silver.

It was a wild rough morning when Samantha woke the following day, but it exactly suited her mood. She got breakfast and when she had washed up, tidied the house and done the few chores necessary in the kitchen, announced her intention of taking a walk. Wrapped in the old tweed coat with its hood pulled carelessly over her hair, she set out along the rough lane leading to the coastguard cottages and Chesil Beach. The last time she had walked that way, she reflected, she had been with Giles and, incredibly, she hadn't liked him overmuch, or, she corrected herself, she had liked him and hadn't wanted to admit it. She hunched her shoulders against the wind and went on down the hill, right to the water's edge, and stood looking across its narrow width to the Beach. Her surroundings were cold and remote, even lonely, but she had no doubt that they were a thousand times better than a mine in Brazil. She had looked up its location in the map the night before and had been shaken to find that the place she was to go to was a good five hundred miles from Rio de Janeiro, and as far as she could judge, surrounded by mountains, a circumstance which normally would have given her some uneasy feelings. As it was, she just didn't care. She turned her back on the water presently and started on the climb back towards the village, composing, as she went, a suitable letter to Antonia, for it was long overdue. It would not, she admitted, be one of the easiest letters to write.

She loitered at the top of the rise, looking down on to the village set in its cosy little valley; she was going to miss it dreadfully. Suddenly the realization of her changed future swept over her; it wouldn't matter where she went, she knew that now. Distance would make no difference; Giles would always be there, the first thing she thought of when she wakened in the morning and her last thought at night. She was, she guessed, one of those tedious people capable of loving only one person—really loving them, and so she would just have to make the best of it and take care not to turn into a nasty-tempered old maid.

She was in the mood for a good cry; it was a pity that at that moment the vicar should appear round the bend of the lane ahead of her. She composed her unhappy face into a semblance of pleasure at meeting him and was appalled to speechlessness when the first thing he asked was: 'And how is that clever young doctor we had staying here? I'm told you've been seeing something of him during your stay in Holland.'

A little surge of anger shook her; life was bad enough without well-meaning people rubbing salt in her wounds; the anger went as quickly as it had come. The vicar was a dear old thing, she wouldn't have hurt his feelings for the world. She began to describe her stay in Dokkum as they walked back to the village together.

She spent the afternoon weeding the garden with a ferocity which played havoc with the young seeds her grandfather had already set, though he, kind old man, said nothing, but watched his patient work being destroyed with his granddaughter's rake and trowel. It certainly tired her out nicely; conscious of her grandparents' anxious looks, Samantha retired to bed early and lay in the dark having the good cry she had been bottling up for far too long. It did her a great deal of good; she slept like a child at last, even though her face was puffy with weeping when she got up the next morning.

After breakfast she went into the kitchen to make jam. Mrs Humphries-Potter had sent over a great deal of the rhubarb which her husband, a gardener of some local repute, forced each year. This early spring it had flourished both early and lavishly, and Samantha, glad of something to do, had undertaken to turn it into jam. Clad in slacks and a sweater, covered with an old-fashioned apron of her grandmother's, tied around her waist with string, she had been busy for half an hour or more, cutting and cleaning the pink sticks. Now she shovelled them into the great copper preserving pan with sugar and lemon rind and ginger, stirred the whole with a large wooden spoon and set it on the Aga to heat up. It was warm in the kitchen and presently the tantalizing smell of boiling jam filled it. Samantha stood over her pan, ready to stir should the need arise, her thoughts far away. With an effort she wrenched them back to reality and the future. She had composed a letter to the mining company that morning, agreeing to attend an interview—the first step, she reminded herself bracingly, in getting a super job at a super salary. The slight drawback represented by her reluctance to go down a mine and her dislike of high mountains were details she would deal with once the job was secured. A wonderful, job, she reiterated to herself, a chance to see the world. She stirred her jam with quite unnecessary vigour and took no notice when the kitchen door was opened and shut again, for her tiresome thoughts had eluded her control once more and had winged themselves back to Haarlem.

'Samantha,' said Giles from across the kitchen, and the world spun round her, so that she dropped the spoon into the jam and jerked round to look in a wild disbelief which almost choked her.

He was leaning against the door, towering to the low ceiling, smiling at her in a way to make her heart melt. Her voice had left her. She framed a soundless Oh because her wits had left her too. When he said:

'Antonia wants to know why you won't come to her wedding,' she just stood staring at him for all the world as though she hadn't heard a word he had said. When she didn't answer, standing there with a face gone white, he went on: 'We all became anxious, you know. Such silence—just a note and then nothing. Tonia telephoned me when I got back and I went to Dokkum...'

She interrupted him then, her voice a little rough and loud: 'I'm going to Brazil.'

'That's a long way to run.' Giles sounded unworried; he appeared the very epitome of careless ease, propping up the door. Samantha ignored him, determined to convince him and herself at the same time. 'It's a super job—down a mine.'

His lips twitched. 'Isn't that a little drastic?' he wanted to know, and crossed the kitchen to remove the bubbling jam from the heat and take her jammy hands in his own. 'My darling,

I cannot allow you to live down a mine for the rest of your life.'

A little colour crept into her cheeks. 'You mustn't talk like that—think of Antonia.'

His black brows rose. 'Antonia? Why should I think of her? Besides, she has Henk to think of her for the rest of their lives.'

'Henk?' Her voice was still too loud and a little shrill, her face quite bewildered.

He looked down at her with love. 'Yes,' he said slowly, 'Henk, my dearest dear, is to marry Tonia. They have been in love for a year or more.' He lifted her hands and kissed them.

'I'm sticky,' said Samantha.

'You're enchanting, my darling girl. And that is the third time I have told you that, and you have never believed me. Do you believe me now?'

'I—I thought you were going to marry Tonia.'

'I cannot imagine why, my darling. I don't remember ever having said so and I'm quite sure she didn't—why, she regards me as another brother, and to me she is a young sister.'

'You took her to Haarlem—you were away all day.'

'Henk—you met Henk?—was on duty at the hospital. I promised that I would fetch Tonia and take her there to see him—it isn't allowed, but we got around that.'

'She could have driven the Mini.'

He smiled a little. 'My love, have you ever seen Tonia drive? She's a menace on the road and a danger to herself.'

Samantha digested this and then: 'You laugh at me,' she accused him.

She was gripped close in his arms. 'Of course I laugh at you—you make me laugh with the delight of seeing you and being with you and talking to you.'

Her voice was very small. 'You might have said so.'

'Indeed I might,' he agreed, 'but your friend Pam was at great pains to tell me—oh, a long time ago—that you were going to marry some-one called Jack. It wasn't until I went to your flat on my way down here that she told me that it was a spur-of-the-moment invention to teach me my place.'

Samantha looked up at his quiet face. 'Yes, they told me. Then why...?'

'Did I not come sooner?' he finished for her. 'I was away, remember? as soon as I had seen Tonia and Sappha I came. I stopped in London for a few hours to attend to certain business. Had you forgotten that I had said no good-byes?'

'I didn't think you meant it.'

'No? And what about this?' He swooped suddenly and caught her fast to kiss her in a fashion which could surely leave no doubt in any girl's mind. 'Do you think that I meant that?'

She had become very pink and her eyes were shining so that she looked almost pretty. 'Oh, Giles, yes!'

'Then here is something else for you to be-lieve, my dearest heart. I love you—I've loved you since the moment you came hurtling through the ward doors at Clement's, firing questions at me like a miniature cannon. I spent time and thought contriving to see you again—Tonia's illness was a godsend, for I was able to arrange for you to nurse her, through old Duggan—and then to get you to Holland. Rolf and Sappha helped, of course—you see, I had to try and make you love me, despite the mythical Jack, and when you treated me so coolly, I was forced to the conclusion that you didn't care for me at all; that I would have to have patience and wait—perhaps for a very long time. And I would have waited, Sam, for the rest of my life, if need be.'

'But supposing I had gone to Brazil?'

'I would have followed you.'

Samantha heaved a sigh, sniffed suddenly and exclaimed: 'The jam! I've forgotten it, it's ruined!'

Giles' hold upon her tightened so that she had the pleasurable sensation that he had no intention of letting her go ever again. 'Dear heart,' he said, 'surely you must agree that it is better to ruin the jam than my life.'

There was only one answer to that, and presently, with her head tucked against his shoulder and her sticky hands clutching the fine cloth of his jacket, she said positively: 'I couldn't bear to ruin your life, Giles.'

He kissed the top of her head, and for a split second, seeing the look on his face, she savoured the future, living in the old house in Haarlem with him, and, in due time, with some small Giles and a daughter or two who wouldn't be plain like their mother, but take after their handsome father. She said out loud, speaking her thoughts: 'I'm a plain girl—you told me so.'

He held her away a little and stared down into her face, studying it with a tender smile.

'You have a lovely face,' he told her. 'You don't have to be pretty to be lovely, you know.'

She thought about this and decided that it was a very satisfactory answer, and when she said so, he murmured: 'That's my girl! Shall we be married tomorrow?'

She caught her breath and choked on it. 'Tomorrow? But I can't—that job—Granny—and I've no clothes.' She thought. 'Besides, you have to have a licence.'

'I have it—the reason for my delay in London,' he smiled down at her. 'The job is soon disposed of, we only have to telephone, and as for your grandmother, she and your grandfather are in the sitting room waiting for us to go and tell them that we are going to be married?'

'How could they possibly know?'

'I did just mention the reason for my visit when I arrived, and I don't fancy that your grandmother was surprised.'

Samantha smiled at him and then reached up to kiss him. 'You think of everything,' she told him admiringly, 'only I still haven't any clothes.'

'We'll go to Weymouth or Dorchester this afternoon. There must be something somewhere to fit you, my darling.'

Men! thought Samantha, with an almost wifely tolerance. Did he really think a girl bought the first dress that fitted her, and her wedding dress at that? But out loud she said in a pleasingly meek voice: 'Yes, dear Giles.'

The jam, simmering richly on the stove, had long since become hopelessly overcooked and unmanageable, the air was thick with its delicious fruitiness; it should really be removed from the stove. The small part of Samantha's mind which had remained practical registered this fact, but only for a brief moment, for Giles was kissing her again.